INITIUM

NATALIE WALTERS

ALSO BY NATALIE WALTERS

Harbored Secrets Series
Living Lies
Deadly Deceit
Silent Shadows

SNAP Agency Series
Initium (novella)
Lights Out (coming November 2021)

A SNAP AGENCY NOVELLA

INITIUM

NATALIE WALTERS

Initium by Natalie Walters

Copyright © 2021 by Natalie Walters

All rights reserved. No part of this book may be reproduced in any form or by any electronic or mechanical means, including information storage and retrieval systems, without written permission from the author, except for the use of brief quotations in a book review.

This is a work of fiction. Names, characters, places, and incidents are products of the author's imagination or are used fictitiously. Any resemblance to actual people (living or dead), organizations, events, and/or locales is purely coincidental.

Cover Design by Kirk DouPonce of DogEared Design

Interior Design by Emilie Haney of EAH Creative

Initium |i-nish-ee-uh-m| (noun) 17th century Latin
• *from the beginning*

CHAPTER ONE

AUGUST 15, 1998
Omagh, Ireland

THE RATTLE of death echoed in his ears. Tom Walsh's fingers trembled as he quickly fed page after page of intel through the shredder. His eyes darted to the distraught but frantic movement of his coworkers around him.

Something had gone wrong.

The intel muddled.

How?

Tom grabbed the Eircell mobile phone off his desk and dialed again. His nerves grew raw at the incessant tone alerting him the call could not go through. Where was Sean? Annie? He tried the home phone number. Their mobile number. But every attempt to reach them was cut off by the annoying tone beeping in his ear.

He checked the volume to make sure the ringer was all the

way up before setting the phone back on the desk. Sean was likely trying to get a hold of them too. Maybe even trying to get to the office. Was that the safest option?

Tom's eyes moved to the Panasonic television mounted in the upper corner of the office. An Ulster Television news anchor, his expression as heavy as his tone, relayed sparse information being fed to him minute by minute.

"Tom, we need to go. Jennings wants us to the safehouse for a debriefing at 1600."

Bob's voice was muted against the thumping of Tom's pulse in his ears. He checked his watch. Half past three. Only twenty-five minutes since the bomb exploded.

A bomb. In Omagh? The explosive concussion had reached their building even a block away, rattling the windows and sending dust drifting down from the hundreds-year-old office building. The team paced after the initial seconds of shock passed, waiting for the call from the Agency. Minutes later, the satellite phone rang. They'd been given their directive: CUT OUT.

The message from the CIA was clear - Byrne Bookkeeping was out of business, at least temporarily. The CIA's mission had potentially been compromised and they needed to get rid of any paperwork that would reveal the actual purpose behind the small accounting firm. Sure, they handled the accounts of a few local companies, but their chief objective was monitoring the activity happening within the rebel paramilitary group known as the Real Irish Republican Army, or RIRA.

The very organization Sean had been working as a double agent.

Why hadn't he contacted them? Had he known about the bomb? Sean had been working with the RIRA for years—secured his position as a trusted associate. So where was he?

INITIUM

Something wasn't right.

"Tom!"

Bob Perkins' frantic tone snapped Tom's attention to his colleague standing two desks over. The man's blond hair was disheveled, his round face red and sweaty.

"Did you hear me?" Bob used his loosened, mustard-colored tie to wipe the sweat beading on his brow. "Are you ready? We need to leave."

Tom continued feeding documents into the shredder. The strips of paper dropped into a burn bag that would be set on fire, permanently destroying any chances their intel would fall into the wrong hands. "Have you heard from Sha—Connor?"

"Oh mercy."

Bob's face paled, his focus shifting back to the television. Tom watched the reporters, now at the scene, just a block over on High Street. The devastation stilled Tom's hands, his breathing, his heart. Black smoke billowed from the buildings where windows, chunks of walls, and whole roofs were blown out. Debris lined the street behind the reporter where medical and police personnel were working the scene, their expressions unable to hide the emotional shock they were witnessing.

Bombs didn't come with warnings...but this one should've. Somewhere, deep in Tom's gut, the weight of that sank heavy. Sean had provided intel a few days ago that the RIRA was gearing up for another attack, but that was the last they heard. Tom and the team continued to monitor the intel, but this morning started out just like every other one—normal. What had they missed?

Tom tore his eyes away from the television screen and fed the last page through the shredder.

"We need to reach Connor and Camille." He was careful to use Sean and Annie's alias'. Given the chaos happening a block over and Sean's warning, he was worried that *if* the CIA's mission in Ireland was compromised it might mean his friends were exposed as well. Had their CIA issued alias' been enough to keep them safe? "I can't leave until I know where they're at. That they're okay."

A flash of compassion passed through Bob's eyes, but he shook his head. "The chief isn't going to let you stay. Protocol." He grabbed the burn bag. "We can try Connor again when we get to the safehouse."

Tom glanced one last time at the television screen. The news camera was zooming in on the charred and disfigured metal skeleton of what was once a car, according to the reporter. Gritting his teeth, Tom grabbed his bag and followed Bob to the van. He had to believe Sean was okay. That just like him, Sean was following protocol and he and Annie would be at the safehouse when they arrived.

TWO HOURS LATER, Tom sat on a lumpy couch in a small one-story cottage forty minutes outside of Omagh in Cookstown. Six CIA officers—including Bob and station chief, Ron Jennings—filled the space around him. Their attention was fixated on the television and the blonde woman reporting the news about the bombing.

Missing and unaccounted for—Sean and Annie.

"They might've been turned back at the checkpoint." The soft words spoken over his shoulder came from Cindy Tate, their finance officer. She tucked a strand of chestnut hair behind her ear. "Told it was safer to stay home."

Leaving when they did had allowed the team to take advantage of the chaos, avoiding the checkpoints now monitoring everyone going in or out of Omagh. Had Sean and Annie been turned back?

INITIUM

"Maybe."

Cindy offered a tentative smile that said she wanted to believe what she was saying but the doubt, the concern, was etched into the fine lines on her forehead.

Jennings twisted the knob on the television turning the volume up. "The IUC Chief cannot come to any conclusion except to say the warning was deliberately misleading..."

"We didn't know." Bob spoke up from the chair nearest the television, looking at Jennings. "The Brits were supposed to be monitoring the calls. We had—"

Jennings held up a hand silencing Bob. "Let's listen."

"It is believed the Real Irish Republic Army is behind the attack, using a car bomb that exploded in front of a busy shopping center. Twenty-six people have died, five are in hospital, which includes women and children."

"We could've stopped it." Tom spoke under his breath. *Should've.* Sean had warned them, but they lacked the intelligence needed to alert officials and now....

The churning in his gut grew worse. He stood and walked to the kitchen table. Six black cell phones were lined up. Each belonging to someone in the house. All were ready to receive the call from Sean or Annie the second they reached out. But they hadn't.

Tom crossed the tiny kitchen and stared out the window over the sink. Guilt pummeled him. What had they missed? The RIRA had increased their attacks and, while America might not be invested in the religious and political concerns between Ireland and Great Britain, it was invested in how the rather small militant group was acquiring resources like weapons, bomb making materials, money, and training.

And somewhere in their trenches was Sean Murphy—an operative for the CIA posing as a member of the RIRA.

One of the phones rang, the sound nearly giving Tom a

heart attack. He spun around and stared at the phones. It wasn't his and the disappointment was crushing. The others quickly joined him, each grabbing their phone and checking. Cindy held hers, casting a quick glance to Tom as she answered it.

The others closed in around her, as anxious for information as Tom was. He rubbed his hands together trying to read Cindy's facial expressions for any tell that—his heart sank. Cindy nodded, her hands to her lips, eyes growing glassy. She cleared her throat and thanked whoever had called. Her shoulders drooped as she looked around at each of them.

"What is it?" Tom nearly shouted. "Who called?"

"It was Tyrone hospital. A few of the victims from the bombing were taken there. Th-they found a card with my name and number on it." Her lips trembled. "It's Annie. She's gone. The baby too."

The world seemed to splinter around Tom, but before he could even digest Cindy's words, Jennings was pushing him toward the front door.

"Get your bags, Walsh, we're leaving Ireland tonight."

"No." Tom stopped short. "We're not leaving without Sean."

Ron Jennings was a good six inches shorter than Tom's own six-two, but that didn't keep the station chief from staring him *down* with narrowed eyes. "You know protocol, Walsh."

"Sir, we can't leave without knowing Sean's status. I'll stay back and—"

"Not happening." Jennings cut him off. The other officers were already heading out of the cottage. "Annie's gone, which means—"

"No, it doesn't." Tom's voice echoed loudly against the sparsely furnished room. "We don't know that Sean is..." the

INITIUM

word lodged in his throat. "We can't leave a man behind unless we know for sure."

Jennings' drill sergeant features softened just a hint. "You don't make the call, Walsh. I do and just like you, I follow orders given to me from the top. We're leaving."

CHAPTER TWO

2013
Washington D.C.

TOM WALSH FROWNED from his lookout on the Francis Scott Key Bridge. The blended sounds of evening traffic and pedestrians passing cancelled out any conversation that might otherwise be overheard from Harbor Pointe, the restaurant below, where Jack Hudson was dining with his family.

In a pair of jeans, t-shirt, and ballcap, Jack's relaxed attire didn't match the strain lining the young man's face. Tom presumed the older woman next to him was Jack's mother from the maternal way she kept running a hand down his cheek or over his arm. Almost like she was checking to make sure he was still there...still okay.

A second later, the woman threw her head back in laughter, the ambient noise muffled the sound but not the joy in her expression or the way it seemed to spread to those sitting at the table with her, and for the first time in the twenty-

INITIUM

minutes or so Tom had been monitoring Jack Hudson, the man smiled.

"You're sure about him?" Tom asked Bob Perkins, who was standing beside him.

"No." Bob sniffed. "He failed the final mission at Peary."

"And he's the first?"

Bob answered Tom's sarcasm with a one shoulder shrug. "If it was easy, everyone would do it."

Tom eyed his friend. He'd aged since Ireland—or maybe it was work adding the lines to his face? "And yet you're suggesting he'd be perfect for my team. Why?"

"It's a nice night." Bob pushed back from the railing and patted his stomach. "Andrea would appreciate it if the reason I'm late to dinner was because I was getting in some exercise."

Tom followed Bob toward the iron stairs that descended from the bridge to the lower level of the Georgetown Waterfront. At the bottom, they joined the other Washingtonians strolling along the Potomac's edge, enjoying the cool October evening.

"He's got a good head. Team leader. Thoughtful." Bob said, as they strolled past the restaurant where Jack and his family were dining on the verandah. "Doesn't have an ego."

Tom couldn't help glancing over to where Jack sat. "And to be a clandestine operative for the CIA, ego is necessary."

A couple got up from a bench and Bob weaved around a family pushing a stroller to get to it. He sat and looked back at Tom. "What?"

"I thought you said Andrea wanted you to get some exercise?"

"I did." Bob smiled. "And now I'm going to stare at the motivation for why I haven't retired yet." He tilted his head to the boats bobbing in the Potomac's current. "Exercising my brain."

Tom looked back at Jack, nearly locking eyes with him before a waiter blocked his view. Joining Bob on the bench, he pretended to be interested in the boats. "Was he military?"

"Nope." Bob answered without any need for explanation.

"Law enforcement?"

"No."

Tom resisted the urge to look over his shoulder, trying to tamp down the feeling that maybe Jack had seen him and was now watching *him*. "So you think a man with no experience, who failed out of the Agency, would be a good fit for my team because he has a good head but no ego. Oh, and he's, what did you say? Thoughtful?"

Bob laughed. "I meant he's not reckless. Thinks things through. Not a knee-jerk reaction kind of fella."

"You've never been subtle, Bob." Tom rubbed his knuckles feeling the tension from twelve years ago tighten around his chest like it was just yesterday. "If you think so highly of him, why didn't you find another place for him in the Agency?"

"I did, but he left." Bob pulled a handkerchief from his pocket and swiped it along his brow, the gesture taking Tom back to that fateful day in Ireland and how it all led to this moment.

"I sent an officer to find him after he failed the final exercise, but he was gone. Packed and already on his way out. Tried to talk to him, but he wasn't really in a talking mood, if you know what I mean, angry. Said he was done. But a few months later I learned he tried to join the FBI."

Tom stood and crossed the walkway to pier's railing, then turned and leaned his back against it, facing Bob. From this position it gave him a good vantage point of Jack without appearing obvious. "What happened with the Fibbies?"

Bob smiled at the FBI nickname. "You'd know if you'd read the dossier."

INITIUM

Bob was right, he hadn't read Jack Hudson's file. Not yet. He wanted to form his own opinion on the man—not read the facts and opinions formed by someone else. Tom knew those weren't always accurate.

Tom kept his eyes on Bob while watching Jack who was slumping in his chair. The young man had to be in his mid-twenties and yet from his posture and the pallor of his skin, even under the peachy glow of the setting sun, he seemed to carry the bearing of someone who'd given up.

Tom wasn't surprised by the reaction to failure. He remembered the excitement and pride of joining the CIA. The honor. Privilege. The rarity of being *chosen*. Had he failed, he'd likely have thrown a pity party for himself too. But, according to Bob, it had been two years since Jack's failed entry into the CIA's clandestine field. Jack Hudson wasn't the first to leave disenchanted when the going got tough and he certainly wouldn't be the last, but did his other qualities make him right for the team Tom was trying to create?

"Not sure I want someone who finds it easy to walk away when things get tough or don't go their way." Tom glanced back at Bob, the memory of his own forced decision searing his conscience. "The assignments will be tough with plans going backwards more times than not."

"Which is why I think Hudson is your man."

Bob's simple statement pushed Tom's attention back to the man sitting at the table. Jack had removed his ballcap and Tom was surprised to see he was bald. Squinting, Tom noticed for the first time the way Jack's clothing seemed to hang on his body. The waitress removed a plate of untouched food from in front of him as he offered up an apologetic smile. An unnerving realization landed heavy in his gut. "He's sick."

"Finished his final chemo treatment two days ago for lymphoma." Bob folded his arms over his chest. "Like I said, after leaving Peary, he applied for the FBI. During his physical they ran his bloodwork and spotted the abnormalities. The diagnosis came quickly after."

"Ending his chances at the FBI." Tom said on a sigh. "A tough blow."

"And yet, he reapplied."

"Which means he might be a little on the stubborn side." Tom studied Jack, recognizing the familiar traits of someone who had battled cancer and the toll it took on the body. Jack looked weak. Tired. But eye-to-eye, would Tom see the same mettle he'd seen in his own sister's eyes in her fight against breast cancer?

"Read his file. You said you were looking for someone for your little *A-Team*. I think he's the perfect Faceman." Bob shot Tom a look. "Maybe a little too much like Faceman."

Tom laughed at Bob's comparison of Jack to the charismatic lady's man from his favorite show. His wife had mailed him the first three seasons of the show on VHS while they were in Ireland and they were played so many times, Tom was certain he could quote every episode verbatim.

The memory of Ireland tempered his mood, reminding him of what brought him to this bridge in the first place. Build a team for his agency—make the world better.

"A little charm could be helpful."

"Or a hinderance." Bob arched a brow. "Don't you want to know how he failed his mission at Peary?"

"Is it important?"

Bob shrugged. "Maybe. Do you plan on having women on your team?"

Tom locked eyes with his friend. "What do you mean?"

"Seems Mr. Hudson had a thing for one of his classmates." Bob checked his watch and rose from the bench, stretching as if the act of sitting was a strain on his muscles. "The instructors

INITIUM

discovered the relationship toward the end and used it to flush them out."

"Flush them out?"

"Come on buddy, you know how it goes. You can't expose your artery and not expect it to be sliced."

Tom controlled the urge to cringe and eyed his friend. Twenty plus years in the agency seeing everything probably made one prone to being unrestrained when it came to the gruesome realities of intelligence. "So you pitted them against one another?"

"Not me personally, but yes. When it came down to the last field exercise test, the instructors pushed them to a decision. They each made a choice."

He'd heard enough. Frustration, decades old, nipped at his nerves. A quick glance back at the restaurant showed an empty table where Jack and his family had been. It was time to go. "I appreciate you reaching out to me."

Bob snorted. "I can't say I like what you're doing. Blackwater has been a thorn in our side for years, getting in the way of missions. Feels like you and this new agency you're trying to form is only going to muddy the waters even more."

"The difference between Blackwater and SNAP is ego. I'm not out here trying to prove something. I want my team to support missions whether it be on a national security level or a private level."

Understanding pulled the skin near Bob's eyes into tight lines. "That wasn't our best day."

"No." Tom said. "And I'd like to offer something to help prevent those days from happening again."

Bob stuck out his hand. "I wish you luck on that. Won't be easy and I know you know it, but if there's anything else you need, well," he smirked. "Don't call me."

Tom winked. "Don't worry, it'll be you calling me next time."

Parting ways, Tom walked to 33rd Street. The sun had set, leaving the street under the fuzzy glow of the orange street lamps. They were spaced too far apart to offer any real light, but he supposed it was more about atmosphere than usefulness. His Mazda was parked at a dark corner near a dumpster. A scuffling noise too big and heavy to be a rodent sounded behind him and the hair on the back of his neck stood.

Pausing, Tom reached his hand toward his pocket as if going for his keys but instead allowed his fingers to brush against the Sig Sauer holstered at his waist. "If you're looking for money, I only carry cards."

"I want to know why you were watching my family."

The voice behind him was low and tempered. Tom's lip twitched. Letting his hand drop, he turned around slowly, showing both of his hands were empty and he was no threat. "Hello, Jack."

Even in the darkness, Tom saw Jack's eyes flash with surprise and then suspicion. "How do you know my name?"

"I know a lot about you, but let's even the field a little." Tom extended a hand. "I'm Thomas Walsh and a good friend of mine suggested you might be interested in a job."

Jack kept his hands poised at his side, his body loose, legs separated in a position that spoke of his self-defense training. "Who's your friend?"

"Bob Perkins."

Another flash of surprise crossed Jack's features before they tightened, eyes narrowing. His shoulders dropped bringing back that posture of defeat Tom had seen earlier. "Not interested."

Tom made his first mistake when he reached for Jack as he turned away. Not all the young man's strength had been stolen

INITIUM

by the chemo, nor his speed. Jack spun out of Tom's reach and landed a hit against his forearm that—had Jack been at his full strength—likely would've broken a bone.

"Stay away from me and my family." Jack's breathless demand revealed that his defensive move had taken its toll on his healing body.

Tom clutched his arm, rubbing his fingers over the skin that would be bruised in the morning. "I'm not with the CIA, Jack. And I don't care what took place at Camp Peary."

They flushed them out, Bob had said. "Actually, that's not true. What happened there is exactly why I think you might be the right man for my team."

"If you know *anything* about me then you know I don't work well with teams."

Jack snorted and then started to turn again.

"Wait." This time Tom didn't approach Jack. He pulled a card out of his pocket. "Take this."

Six heartbeats passed before Jack took the offered card. He read it and looked up. "SNAP?"

"Strategic Neutralization and Protection Agency." Tom explained the acronym. "It's a private contract agency created to neutralize threats as quickly as possible in order to protect our country as well as the every-day American."

"*Strategically?*"

Tom smiled. Jack was smart and had a quick wit. "Yes, and I'm strategically building my team and looking for a leader. You—"

"Nope." Jack shook his head and handed the card back, but Tom refused it. "Either you're a liar or dense. You don't dress like someone who has risotto for brains, but I'd hate to call you a liar."

"I'm not a liar."

Jack took a step closer, putting him eye to eye with Tom.

"Then you'd know that I failed out of Camp Peary, put my entire team and the mission at risk. You'd also know that a month before I was supposed to join the FBI, I was told I had cancer. If you knew all about me like you first claimed, you'd know that I grew up attending church with my family until I was eighteen. I even attended service occasionally throughout college.

"But more than that, you'd know that even if I wanted to find out more about your snappy named agency, God has made it clear to me that I'm not cut out for a role protecting our country or anyone in it."

The anger, frustration, and pain were clear in Jack's words and tone. Tom recognized the helplessness. He'd felt it too.

"Or," Tom countered. "God might've been preparing you for this moment here."

Tom hadn't grown up in the church like Jack and had once had a hard time wrapping his mind around a God who had the power to control the world but still allowed atrocities to happen. So he could imagine it was that much harder for someone like Jack.

Then Omagh had happened. Sean. Annie. Tom had every reason to believe God couldn't exist and yet...he'd been proven wrong. Attending church—reading his Bible—he wanted to say he had a better understanding of how God worked, but that wasn't true. Still, he *had* learned to trust, and now Tom needed Jack to do the same.

"I can't say I understand what you're going through or have been through, but I know what I'm looking for." Tom backed towards his car. "I have a job coming up in a few weeks. If you're interested in testing your theory about whether or not you're really cut out to be a protector—my *snappy* number is on the card."

Jack arched a brow but didn't say anything, so Tom turned,

INITIUM

pressed his key fob to unlock the door and got in. In his rearview mirror, he saw Jack read the card again, shoving it into his back pocket before walking away.

Tom blew out a breath and prayed he was doing the right thing. He had a feeling many lives were going to depend on it.

CHAPTER THREE

AUGUST 16, 1998
Langley, VA

"SHE'S DEAD. THEY KILLED ANNIE." Tom sucked in a frustrated breath. He stared out over the Virginia landscape outside of CIA headquarters, the normally calming view doing nothing to settle his agitation. "We can't leave Sean there."

"We don't even know if he's alive, Walsh." Ron Jennings sat against his desk, arms folded over his chest. "The situation in Omagh is too hot right now."

Not as hot as he was. If an outburst at the small Irish airport wouldn't have put the rest of the Omagh team in danger, Tom wouldn't have gotten on the plane that brought them home. He would've demanded that one of them stay back and search for Sean until they knew his fate for certain.

"When can we go back?"

"The CIA Director is working closely with the President and—"

INITIUM

"Doing nothing." Tom fumed. "We've been here for weeks, which means Sean's life isn't a priority and neither was Annie's...."

He swallowed the emotion that came up every time he thought of Sean's pregnant wife. His mind immediately went to Samantha and his reluctance to ask her to marry him. It wasn't cold feet that held him back, but a different kind of fear.

At thirty-eight, Tom had long since accepted that his job with the CIA was the only intimate relationship he'd know, but then a chance meeting with Samantha Mills at a work party two years ago changed everything. Driven and intelligent, Sam's position working directly for the Deputy Director of the National Security Agency spoke of her dedication and commitment to her job over all else in her life, including relationships, as she'd admitted over a steak dinner on their second date. It was on their third date, over a bowl of chocolate fudge brownie ice cream and an obscene amount of maraschino cherries, that Tom felt an undeniable desire well within him that *this* woman was meant just for him.

The odds weren't in their favor for a successful relationship, given their careers in the intelligence field. They both worked unpredictable hours, had unexpected trips that, at least for him, kept him away for an indeterminable amount of time based on the mission, and for the most part neither one of them could discuss what they were working on. Which, he thought, might've been a good thing seeing as how she'd understand the extended absences, the growing number of stress lines spreading across his face, and the unexplainable injuries that sometimes occurred when the mission went awry.

Asking Sam to marry him meant she'd have to accept the uncertainty of his job—a conversation they had many times, to which she always assured him that she was prepared for the risks associated with his career in the CIA. And so he asked—and she said yes.

Those earlier fears he'd had before they were engaged reared back up as Tom read the reports coming in. Details of those killed and injured in the bombing. A fifteen-year-old girl, who dreamed of being a pianist, now blind. A young mother in a coma unaware that her toddler had been killed. School-aged children, shop owners, volunteers, and Annie. The acknowledgement of her death along with that of her unborn baby made for especially painful headlines.

Headlines Tom couldn't help seeking out. Since landing in the U.S., he'd become obsessed with all the news coverage, watching CNN, BBC, pulling up foreign reports, monitoring every bit of chatter coming out of Ireland—searching the video and photo images for Sean.

"Sean not only lost his wife," Tom looked up at Jennings. "He lost his children. We owe it to them to bring him back home."

"You were in the debriefing with me, Tom." Jennings stood. "*If* Sean is alive then the last thing we want to do is expose him. The Royal Ulster Constabulary wasn't wrong. The warnings were inaccurate. They literally sent the crowds toward the bomb and they're blaming us and Britain for having intel beforehand and not doing something about it."

Outside of Jennings' office, the intelligence officers from Omagh were scrambling to figure out what had gone wrong. Trying to find a reason behind the miscommunication of information that had caused the Irish police force to unknowingly move people towards the bomb instead of away.

Tom slipped off his glasses and rubbed the bridge of his nose. "Sean tried to warn us. He called and told us there was going to be a bombing. If he'd known more than that he would've told us."

INITIUM

Straightening from his repose against the desk, Jennings pressed his lips together and moved to the coffee station at the corner of the conference room, which was also being used as a makeshift command post for their team. Tom got the feeling there was something behind the station chief's quiet apprehension.

"What is it?"

"An intel report came in last night." Jennings added sugar to his coffee, stirred, then took a sip before continuing. "I didn't want to mention anything until I had more information, but maybe knowing this will make you understand the agency's hesitancy."

Hesitancy? Tom felt his breathing grow shallow.

"Suspicion is growing around Sean's involvement." Jennings continued after another cringe-worthy sip. "MI5 believes Sean was the one behind the construction of the bomb that was placed inside the car. And that he was the one behind the miscommunication."

"Impossible." Tom shot out of his chair, pulse pounding in his ears. "There's no way Sean would turn on us. On Annie. The Brits are just trying to cover their own backsides."

"Maybe, but until we get more intel we have to proceed with caution regarding Sean's status."

Tom's blood pressure was rising. "All the more reason why we should be back there. We don't know if Sean was discovered. Killed." He didn't want to accept that Sean would defect but if the Real IRA found out he was a double agent, if they'd used Annie against him...how far would Sean go to keep her safe?

"We never should've left. It was a mistake, and we need to get back there now."

Jennings shook his head. "When things settle, maybe we can send a team back to Ireland."

Tom scoffed. "And how long will that be?"

Jennings offered no answer.

"So, we're just supposed to sit here and leave Sean's parents, his sister, wondering why he just dropped off the face of the earth?" He grit his teeth. "Or worse, we're going to allow unverified intel to paint Sean as a traitor and murderer? We're supposed to believe that Sean went rogue? Defected and allowed his wife and unborn child to—"

"There's nothing we can do."

Tom pounded his fist against the table. "That's bull and you know it."

Jennings didn't flinch, his composed posture somehow leveling the turbulent emotion and forcing Tom to take a breath. "We have teams in the U.K. even other parts of Ireland that can go in and—"

"No." Jennings's sharp tone cut him off. The soft lines of his face hardened into resolve. "There's more at play here. And until we figure out what it is, we are to hold steady here in the U.S."

"Send me." Tom said, his voice surprisingly calm. "You and I both know Sean wouldn't turn, so send me back. I'll stay low, reach out to a few informants, and report back to you. We can't abandon him there, not after everything he's lost."

"I won't remind you that Sean knew the risks of the job and willingly accepted them the same as you and I did. He was lucky the agency didn't take action when Annie came into the picture, but she was good for the story—"

"The story? Listen to yourself, Jennings. This isn't a story. This is a man's life—one of our own—we're talking about. Point to the part in our manuals where it says we turn our back on one another."

Something close to pity crossed Jennings's features before he spoke. "You know the mission comes first."

INITIUM

The sounds around him grew muted, the office space turned hazy. *The mission comes first.* It was a truth instilled in them from their very first days at the Agency, but no one really understood the weight of it until pushed to a decision. Decisions that usually affected the lives of others. Samantha's smile, and the way it transformed her whole face causing her vibrant blue eyes to sparkle, filled his mind.

Reaching for his glasses, Tom thought about the ring again. One day soon he would vow to love and honor Sam all the days of their lives. Tom wouldn't allow a mission-first decision to steal Sam's beautiful smile or the life they could have together. He had a choice right now to do that. Unlike Sean.

"You're sure there's no way you can send me back?" he asked, already knowing the answer.

Jennings shook his head. "I'm sorry but that's no longer the mission."

Releasing a sigh, Tom unclipped his ID badge and set it on the table in front of Jennings.

"I no longer want to be part of that mission."

CHAPTER FOUR

AUGUST 24, 1998
Alexandria, Virginia

TOM MUTED THE TELEVISION, twisting his attention to Sam. She was reading a biography on Nelson Mandela, the remnants of their date—takeout containers—still sitting on the coffee table. Under the glow of the late-night news washing his townhouse in a blue hue, he imagined married life wouldn't be much different than this. Or at least he hoped.

Did Sean and Annie share nights like this?

"Do you think he's alive?" he asked.

Sam looked up from her book for a second before placing a bookmark between the pages and scooting next to him. She ran her hand down the back of his head, her fingers working their way through his hair until they reached his neck with a gentle massage. "I'm praying."

Tom felt the muscles in his neck tighten under her touch. He reached back and gently took her hand into his. His

INITIUM

thumb brushed against the ring on her finger. "Praying for what?"

She glanced at him, the gray in her blue eyes darker today. "What do you mean?"

"It's been almost two weeks," Tom pointed the remote at the news droning from their television, "since the bombing in Omagh and there's nothing about it. It's like what happened in Ireland is irrelevant in the face of our president and his scandalous behavior in the White House."

Tom flipped through the cable channels until he found BBC. He groaned. The whole world was captivated by the president's immoral behavior, meanwhile somewhere in Northern Ireland Sean could be dead. Or alive. Tortured?

"Do I pray for him to be alive, knowing we just left him there or do I pray for..." Angry emotion balled in his throat.

Sam's hand found his and she interlaced their fingers before resting her head on his shoulder. "We just pray."

Her words were soft against the noise droning from the television and yet unfaltering. Of the two, she carried more faith than he did. It was one more area in his life where Sam had intricately woven herself into his being. Attending church wasn't something his parents prioritized, only attending on the occasional Sunday or holidays. They'd allowed him to decide for himself if he wanted to go, and with sports, homework, and late nights out with friends on Saturdays, getting up early on a Sunday morning to sit through an hour-long sermon wasn't high on his list of priorities. Not much had changed once he joined the CIA. Unlike God, the agency worked seven days a week.

When Sam asked him to go to church with her the first time, he'd felt guilty that he was doing it more for her than for his soul. But it didn't take long before Pastor Marty's words opened something inside of Tom—an emptiness that was only filled when he attended service, or read the Bible with Sam, or prayed.

Just pray.

It was such a simple thing to do and yet it didn't feel like enough. Tom couldn't ignore the guilt that grew with each passing day—he should've done more. He shouldn't have left Ireland without Sean. What if more intel had come in proving MI5's report wrong? He should've fought Jennings harder. Pushed back until a plan was formed to go back and find out the truth.

He shouldn't have quit.

Tom's gut twisted. He didn't regret quitting the agency, but in the weeks since his sudden departure he had questioned his impulsivity. Outside of agency employment, he was left in the dark abyss of the unknown. His emotional reaction had cost him the last connection he had to Sean. If he had stayed a little longer he might've been able to keep the pressure on Jennings and the Directorate of Operations.

The echo of the doorbell cut into his thoughts. He and Sam sat forward on the couch, Sam's expression wordlessly asking if he was expecting someone. Tom shook his head and shrugged.

"I'll clean this up." Sam set her book aside and began collecting foam containers from their dinner.

Tom kissed his fiancée's forehead before heading to his door. Who could be coming at this late hour? Even when employed with the CIA he hadn't received late night visitors. His shoulders relaxed as he spotted the familiar face through the peephole. Twisting the bolts, he unlocked his door, and opened it to greet his friend.

"Well, if it isn't Reuben Jones."

His friend smiled wide from the porch. "Glad to see retirement from the Agency hasn't pushed you into an early sleep pattern."

INITIUM

"I'm too young to retire and—"

"And too stubborn to know better." Reuben cut in. "I hear that, man." He peered into the foyer of the townhouse. "I'm sorry for just showing up but..."

Tom waved Reuben in, watching the Michael Jordan look-alike duck as he stepped inside.

His deep set eyes searched the space again. "I have a job you might be interested in."

"Evening, Reuben." Sam walked up carrying her book and her laptop. "How are April and the kids?"

"Firecrackers, all of them." Reuben answered on a laugh. "I'm sorry for stopping by so late."

"That's okay, I was just getting ready to head out." She slid her computer into her bag and looked over at them. "Should I put a pot of coffee on?"

Reuben shook his head. "I'm good. I turn forty and April has me drinking decaf now and I'm not sure what the point is. Might as well drink water."

Sam laughed and then pressed a kiss to Tom's cheek. "Don't stay up too late."

He squeezed her hand. "Call me when you get home."

He watched her walk to her car, and give a quick wave before driving off. Closing the door, he felt her absence hollow him. It was getting harder and harder to watch her leave. He made a mental note to talk with her in the morning and bring up a short engagement again.

Tom's curiosity silenced the wedding bells tolling in his mind as he led Reuben to the living area. He'd first met the man five years before when Reuben was working as the head regional security officer for the U.S. ambassador in Turkey. Reuben was a former State Trooper for Virginia and he'd brought that experience to his job with the diplomatic security attaché. If he was here to recruit Tom to the State Department, he'd wasted the trip.

"I'm sorry to hear about the embassies." Tom said after they sat. "Did you know anyone?"

"Not this time." Reuben didn't sit back but rather perched himself at the edge of the wingback chair, elbows on knees, expression thoughtful. "I'm grateful the U.S. responded though."

A week before the bombing in Omagh, two American embassies had been bombed in Tanzania and Kenya. In response, America sent missile strikes against several of Osama Bin Laden's camps in what they were calling Operation Infinite Reach.

In an instant, Tom was transported back to the little bookkeeping shop on Market Street, the smell of burnt metal and rubber permeating his senses as if he was standing right there again. "I hope we're ready for their response. When do you go back?"

"I don't. I left State three months ago. It's why I'm here." Reuben shifted in his seat. "I heard about Sean." His eyes lowered for a moment before looking back up. "And Annie."

Every muscle in Tom's body went rigid. Sean's position in Ireland was classified. No one, not even his family, had been given information on Sean's status. "How?"

"I'm part of a team and we have...connections that make us privy to high-level security insight."

Tom clamped his teeth down, confusion rivaled with indignation that Sean's mission had been compromised. "What kind of *team* has connections to top secret missions within the CIA?"

"The kind that's hired to protect assets critical to the security of the nation."

A bell went off in his head. Last year a private military

INITIUM

company, *Blackwater*, had been started by a former Navy SEAL. Tom heard rumors about this rogue organization. Some of his colleagues were worried that with its access to intel and highly trained contractors, without guidance of any governing entity, they might disrupt the CIA's operations.

"If you're here to get information from me—"

"I know you better than that," Reuben interrupted, a crease between his brows. "I'm here because a job just came up and I thought maybe you'd like to assist us."

Tom let a few seconds of silence spread between them as intuition urged him to be cautious. *Everyone* was seeking information whether they admitted it or masked it as a favor of assistance. "What kind of assistance do you need?"

Reuben placed his hands on his knees. "The Donahue family is from Tennessee. They own Donahue Oil Company and are worth almost half a billion dollars. Three days ago, they received an email containing a photo of their son, William. A phone call followed with the demand for five million Irish pounds. Almost seven million U.S."

Tom's pulse picked up. "Irish pounds?"

"Bill Donahue, William's father, sent his son to Ireland as a graduation present. He left a pub in Belfast and we believe he was stopped at what was set up as a Gardaí checkpoint where he was taken at gunpoint."

"Who has him?"

"The Real IRA." Reuben's tone was measured. "We leave in the morning to go get him."

"Extract him, you mean."

Rueben gave a subtle nod.

"And you need me?"

"I'm handling logistics and we've got a few former Special Ops soldiers taking care of the tactical aspect, but you know the area. You know how they operate."

There was more. Tom felt it in his gut even if Reuben wasn't saying it. "And?"

"We have a guy on the ground. He sent us this." Reuben reached into his back pocket, pulled out a folded 8x11 photo, and handed it to Tom.

The image was grainy at best but the face staring back at him looked too familiar to be a coincidence. "Sean?"

"We don't know for sure, but I figured you'd know about that too." Reuben pressed his lips together before speaking. "We have space for one more if you're interested."

Tom looked at the image again. He exhaled slowly, thinking about Sam's simple request. *Just pray.* Even the way she said it held the kind of confidence that exuded peace. The kind of peace Tom so desperately wanted to feel but feared he wouldn't know until he found out what happened to Sean.

"There's one thing you should know before you make your decision," Reuben said quietly. "This mission isn't sanctioned."

Having worked in the CIA long enough, Tom understood what that meant. No one would know why they were going to Ireland, which meant there'd be no backup if things went sideways. He thought of Sam, and what it would mean if the worst happened. He inhaled a slow breath and held out his hand. "I'm in."

CHAPTER FIVE

2015
Washington D.C.

"SIR, WE HAVE A SITUATION."

Tom pulled his attention from the computer screen to meet Jack Hudson's concerned gaze. "What's going on?"

Jack stepped into Tom's office and made a face. "Paint's still not dry?"

Tom waved off his comment. "Tell me what's going on."

"It's Lyla, I think she has a death wish."

Tom's shoulders relaxed just a fraction. "Is that all? Why do you think I asked you to keep an eye on her a few years back?"

"I know. But the girl is crazy." Jack blushed. "Sorry, sir, I know you're close to her and her family."

"It's the truth," Tom said as he signed an invoice for the computer equipment he'd purchased for the state of the-art tech set-up that would become the hub for the agency's office just outside his own glass-walled space. For now, it was still a bunch of desks and dark computer terminals. "What's she done this time?"

"It's not what she's done, exactly." Jack's brow furrowed. "Do you remember the Travis case you had me working when I first joined?"

Three years and the Travis case still made Tom's blood run cold. Tom prayed fervently that a very special place in hell was prepared for those involved in child sex-trafficking. "What does that case have to do with Lyla?"

"A member of the FBI team we worked with back then reached out to me a few days ago. Said there's a rumor that gang members involved in the trafficking might've started up the business again. Only this time they've found a loophole."

"What's that?"

"College students."

Time seemed to still as Tom searched Jack's worried expression. "Lyla?"

"No." Jack shook his head. "She's not involved...yet."

It had only taken a few days to understand what Bob Perkins meant when he said Jack was deliberate in his actions back when Tom first asked the younger man to join his newly established team. A bit of an opposite to Tom's own knee-jerk personality, Jack's method felt like someone trying to be gentle when pulling off the bandage. Tom needed it to be ripped off.

"Spit it out, Jack."

"There's a prostitution ring of sorts taking place at several colleges around the country. Here in D.C., in Virginia. And at Glendale. The FBI sent me some photos to see if I could identify any key players from our case." Jack grimaced. "There's a photo of Lyla."

Tom was nauseous. "Is that why you've been leaving work?"

INITIUM

"I wanted to be sure before I brought it to your attention. You know how she is."

He did. Since the day she was born, Tom knew this little girl was going to be a force to be reckoned with. Being asked to be Lyla's godparent was an honor that came with heavy responsibility. Especially knowing she would always be the closest thing he'd ever get to having a child of his own.

Guilt racked him. It shouldn't be Jack telling him that something was going on with Lyla. Tom should've been watching her himself. But with getting SNAP up and running, or rather, more organized, his time had been consumed. As it was, his tiny agency was already at capacity for their assignments. Hiring Jack had been a great decision, but one that left him turning down more opportunities until he could hire more team members.

"It seems one of Lyla's classmates might be involved in this escort ring. According to the FBI, Lyla was confronting one of the men who had taken his frustration out on her friend's face. I don't think she knew what the situation was, but sir," Jack ran a hand through hair that had grown in thick and dark since finishing chemo. "The man her friend was with was a senator from Illinois."

"Please don't tell me—"

"Craig Donaldson."

Tom ran a hand down his face. Senator Donaldson was rumored to be involved with the Chicago Syndicate, a nasty group of mobsters deeply imbedded in the Teamsters Union that had a reputation for getting their way or getting people *out* of their way.

Oh, Lyla. Why do you have to be so strong-willed and defiant?

Tom's desk pressed into his chest as he leaned forward. "Have you heard anything specific?"

"I put out a few feelers to see if there's anything out there. I don't think Lyla knows who Senator Donaldson is, but she did snap a photo of him, threatening to inform the police."

"Good grief."

"Yeah, not good." Jack concurred. "I put a detail on Lyla's apartment since the incident. There's been a car parked outside that leaves when she does and returns when she does. I ran the license plate already." He slid a piece of paper across the desk with a photo on it. "James Nicoletti."

Tom looked at Jack. "Who is he?"

"The nephew of Johnny Nicoletti. A source in Chicago said the kid's trying to earn his chops hoping to take over a part of the Chicago district."

"So he's motivated to prove himself." Tom pinched the bridge of his nose.

"Yes, but so far it appears he's content just to watch her. I think they're waiting to see what Lyla does."

"Or they know who she is and who her parents are." Tom added. "Looks like I'll be joining my goddaughter and her parents for dinner tonight."

"Good luck, sir." Jack gave a two-finger salute. "If you need anything else let me know."

AN HOUR AND A HALF LATER, Tom had spoken with his best friend and confirmed that Lyla was expected home for dinner that night. He pulled into the long drive towards the six thousand square foot house that sat nestled among the tall trees on a sprawling hundred-and-fifty-acre property in the Virginia mountains. Keith Fox had done well in the tech industry, but at least half of his wealth had come with his marriage to Catherine.

Aside from their sprawling residence, no one would know

INITIUM

the wealth of Keith and Catherine by their character. They didn't drive exotic cars or wear clothing with brand name labels. They volunteered, donated, and led quiet lives...which made Lyla's personality stand out. Strong-willed was putting it mildly, but Keith and Catherine showered her with equal parts love and discipline, and were careful not to over-indulge her too much.

However, Lyla was known to toe the line. He parked next to the BMW M8 and saw a physics textbook in the passenger seat.

Tom pressed the doorbell and was surprised to see the housekeeper, Annabelle, answer it. "Sir, thank goodness you are here." The panic etched deep in her face sent Tom's heart galloping in his chest.

"What's wrong?"

Before the housekeeper could answer, Keith rounded the corner of the hallway coming out of the kitchen, his face pale. "Lyla's gone."

"What do you mean, gone?"

"Catherine saw her pull into the drive but when she didn't come in right away, she checked on her and saw Lyla talking to someone on her cell phone. She seemed upset. Catherine took a call of her own, and when she got off, Lyla was gone."

If not for his conversation with Jack, Tom might've assumed this was typical Lyla behavior, but his instinct warned him to be worried. "Have you tried calling her?"

"Yes, but it just goes to voicemail. Catherine wants to call the police, but I think that's a bit of an overreaction." Keith's eyes searched Tom, as if waiting for affirmation of his opinion.

They'd known each other since childhood, both growing up in plain, two bedroom homes on Madison Street, where they played cops and businessmen. The main difference between their families was that Tom's father was a blue-collar worker for

RLA Steel Company and Keith's father was a savvy investor who *lived* like a blue collar. Not a single neighbor knew of their wealth that reached well into seven figures. Like his father, Keith was smart. Instead of only investing money, which he did, he also invested his skills in the early years of the tech industry, eventually creating Fox Technologies at the age of twenty-nine and dominating in his field.

Tom had always known Keith to be calm and collected, but he could see the deep lines of worry cutting across his friend's brow, breaking his normally composed exterior.

"Tom, you don't think we should call the police, do you?"

"No." He put a hand on Keith's shoulder. "Let me try and see if I can get a hold of her."

Keith nodded, a small measure of relief loosening the taut lines on his forehead.

"Can you forward me the security footage from when she was here?"

Keith pulled out his cell phone and was already typing as he nodded. "Yes."

A second later, Tom's phone pinged with the information. He checked it and watched Lyla pull in, get out of her car, answer a call, her face morphing into confusion, then concern, before it hit anger and then...determination.

Oh, Lyla, what are you up to?

A minute later, someone in a black Porche picked her up and took off. According to the time on the surveillance video the whole thing happened within ten minutes, which meant the Porche's driver was somewhere close when they called, assuming the caller and driver were the same person.

Tom clicked through the different angles of the cameras that surrounded the property until he found the one directed at the front gate of the home and the street. His shoulders relaxed to find there was no sign of the car that Jack had spotted tailing Lyla. Maybe this really was just a typical Lyla move.

"Do you know who owns the Porche?"

Keith shook his head. "No. It could be any one of her friends though. Lyla's smart enough not to get into a stranger's car."

Again, Keith's inflection hinged on it being a statement that he needed Tom to support. To assure him Lyla was okay. Tom couldn't—wouldn't—make any promises. Not with all that he'd witnessed working as a contract security officer.

"I'm going to take this and get some guys to look into the license plate. See if we can get information about the driver." Tom was backing away towards the front door. "You stay here with Catherine and keep trying to call Lyla. If you hear *anything* or Lyla returns, let me know. Until then, hang tight. Let me see what I can do."

Before he could step out the door Keith stopped him by grabbing his elbow and pulling Tom into a fierce hug.

"I don't know everything you do, but I trust you to make sure my baby girl is safe."

Emotion balled at the back of Tom's throat. When Keith pulled back, his eyes were rimmed red and desperate.

"I'll bring her home." Tom set his jaw and turned on his heel. Outside of the stately mansion, he slid inside his car, cell phone already ringing with the call he'd just placed.

"Jack. I need you back at the office and running down every lead you have on Senator Donaldson and James Nicoletti. And find out if the Chicago Syndicate is operating in D.C. Lyla's gone."

CHAPTER SIX

AUGUST 25, 1998
Belfast, Ireland

A THICK FOG had rolled in, blanketing the green hills of Black Mountain, and spreading across Belfast like a bad omen. Tom had expected he'd feel at home once the Nextant400XTI landed, but an unsettling feeling stirred his soul the second his foot hit the tarmac of the tiny airport.

It was too late to question his decision to join *the team*, consisting of one other man Tom had barely been introduced to before a quick briefing, which concluded shortly after their backsides hit the leather seats on the private jet. The man, apparently, didn't take issue with going into a mission with someone he'd just met. Tom wasn't sure if that was reassuring or not.

Breathing in the damp night air, Tom closed his eyes and thought of Sam. He'd kept the details of the trip vague. He didn't want to put Sam or her job with the National Security

INITIUM

Agency at risk by giving her too much information. But Sam was smart. One look into her blue eyes and Tom knew she knew there was more to this trip than gathering information about Sean. And yet, she still gave him her full support.

If she hadn't, he wouldn't have come...right? When he worked for the CIA, he knew the line of work he was involved in, and it had kept him from any meaningful relationship. He hated to admit it, but Director Jennings had been right. Every intelligence officer knew what they were signing up for when they joined the CIA.

But this wasn't the CIA. This was a team of five outfitting themselves in Kevlar and arming themselves for an unauthorized mission.

"You ready?"

Tom opened his eyes and looked over at Reuben, who was standing next to him. He wore a dark blue jumpsuit with a fish logo on it and a black beanie cap pulled over his head.

Was anyone ever ready to step into the unknown? The story of Peter from the Bible flashed to mind. The disciple stepped out of the boat and onto the raging sea to meet Jesus, only to be sunk by his fears. Jesus grabbed Peter's hand and asked him why he doubted. Was Tom doubting his purpose here?

"Tom?" Reuben asked again, concern cutting lines across his forehead. "You ready, man?"

Thunder rumbled in the distance.

"Yeah." Tom tucked the Sig Sauer P226 into the holster at the back of his waist. The familiar weight was a comfort, as were Samantha's soft words, whispered into his ear as they'd said goodbye. *Trust God and pray.*

Still new in his faith, Tom questioned if it was too much to believe God might've given him this opportunity to return to

Ireland? Find Sean? Or at least find closure? Was that selfish? *Not if Sean was alive and he could bring him home.*

Tom followed Reuben across the tarmac to the small van with the words O'Malley's Fish on the side. Based on the pungent fish odor, Tom was certain the vehicle still operated as such. The team of five climbed into the back.

"Oi, I'll be smelling like carp for a month." Liam Kelly, the man sitting across from Tom made a face. "Couldn't find us a Gat truck, eh?"

He was speaking to the driver, Patrick O'Donnell. Of the team, these two were members of the Gardaí; the Irish police force. They had been working with Roger Briggs, a former Special Forces officer for the U.S., here in Belfast for the last year. Tom had met him briefly before he took off ahead of them to run surveillance on the property they were headed to now. Next to Reuben was the fifth member, and the one who'd traveled with them to Ireland early that morning, Joe Mitchell. Also Special Forces, he was the point-man for this operation and the contact between the Donahue family and the kidnapper.

With their Irish brogue so thick it could barely count as discernable, Patrick and Liam's banter filled the quiet of the van as they traveled across the Irish landscape for the next two hours. Between the fish odor, his nerves, and the van bouncing along the rutted farmland road, Tom began to feel green about the gills, but when the vehicle finally began to slow, the nausea knotting his stomach eased.

Peeking through the windshield, he caught a glimpse of the fortified stone wall surrounding the Northern Irish town of Derry. He checked his watch. Nearly eight in the evening. Most families would be home from work and finishing up supper.

Though some might still be out enjoying the extended

INITIUM

hours of sunlight still brightening the sky at the late hour; a scenario they'd considered. According to Mitchell, Briggs' team had tracked two of the kidnappers, which Tom had identified as members of the Real IRA, to the small farming village of Hillsford, a few kilometers outside of Derry. The van stopped. Tom reached for the door handle, anxious to suck in a breath of fresh air, but Mitchell caught his hand.

"You know the plan?"

Tom slid a sideways glance at Reuben and then back to Mitchell. "Yes. You want names of anyone else I recognize as members of the RIRA."

"And anyone else of significance." Mitchell said, staring Tom down a few seconds longer before releasing his hand and twisting the silver handle back and sliding the van door open.

Mitchell got out first, followed by Kelly. Reuben gave Tom a supportive pat on the shoulder before joining the others. Rubbing sweaty palms down the front of his jeans, Tom thought of Sean. Only Reuben knew of his connection to the CIA. Tom guessed Mitchell and Briggs were smart enough to figure it out. But Kelly and O'Donnell...they saw Sean as a suspect for the Omagh bombing, which would put him in their crosshairs.

Tom slipped in the ear piece, weighing the situation. He had to get to Sean first.

The call came in from Briggs that two of the four suspects holding William Donahue had left for the ransom drop. Tom, Kelly, O'Donnell, and Mitchell began their approach towards the small thatched-roof cottage while Reuben remained with the van, keeping it ready for their quick departure.

Fanning out under the cover of Ash and Hawthorn trees, Kelly and O'Donnell took point, while Mitchell led Tom around the back.

Mitchell held a closed fist up at a half wall a few feet from the back door. Tom slowed his breathing and waited. Except for the crickets warming up for their nightly symphony, all was quiet.

"When we get in there," Mitchell whispered. "I want you to—"

Before he could finish, an eruption of gunfire coming from the front of the house cut him off. Tom dropped into a squat out of instinct as more gunfire and shouting filled the night air. Mitchell was already running in a crouched position towards the back door. Pulse pounding, Tom whipped his gun out and leveled it in front of him as he followed. Already at the house, Mitchell's boot slammed into the door, nearly jarring it off its hinges.

Continued shouting and gunfire gave them the cover they needed to enter the home unnoticed. A single wall separated the front room from the kitchen. To their left was another room, a padlock on the door. Mitchell gave a nod and then approached it as Tom kept cover. Another well-timed kick and the door swung inward. Mitchell disappeared inside and emerged two agonizing minutes later with a disheveled-looking William Donahue.

Backtracking, they exited the home and hustled towards the waiting van. Gunfire continued to pepper the air and Tom felt pulled to turnaround and help Kelly and O'Donnell.

"Get in," Reuben shouted from the driver's seat. "The Gardaí is on their way."

"Wait." Tom hesitated. He looked back at the house. Was Sean inside? There had been no time to check. "I've gotta go back."

"Kid's the mission." Mitchell said, looking at Reuben. "Let's move out."

Frustration throbbed in sync with the chaotic staccato of

INITIUM

the gunfire happening behind him. Sirens echoed nearby reminding Tom there would be no explanation for his presence. Staying wouldn't just blow Reuben's mission, it'd expose Tom's reason for being in Ireland in the first place. And *that* would expose Sean if he was still imbedded with the RIRA...or alive.

"Come on, man. We don't even know if he's in there." Reuben slapped his hand against the steering wheel. "Think about Samantha, brother."

It was an unfair tactic and Reuben's apologetic expression said he knew it, but it was enough. Without a word, Tom jumped into the van. *This was not how it was supposed to go.*

Mitchell slammed the door shut as Reuben hit the gas. The van sped down the bumpy road, as Tom let his head fall into his hands, praying for Kelly and O'Donnell. And hoping he wasn't leaving his friend behind, again.

CHAPTER SEVEN

AUGUST 25, 1998
Dublin, Ireland

"THEY KNEW what they signed on for."

Tom looked up from the bathroom sink and shut off the faucet. He grabbed the washcloth from the towel rack and wiped the hot water dripping off his face before staring at Reuben. His colleague's words didn't sit well with him. They were too close to the ones spoken to him by Director Jennings two weeks ago.

"No one signs up to die."

Tom balled the washcloth and threw it on the counter of the tiny motel room they'd checked into a half hour ago. The worn green carpet matched the dark green bedspread with clovers across it and Tom guessed it was to immerse visitors in the emerald isle but the dingy room just made him feel worse. Halfway into their two-hour drive from Belfast to Dublin they received word that Kelly had been killed in the gunfight. O'Donnell was in critical condition at a hospital. Neither of the apprehended suspects were Sean, but it didn't make Tom feel any better about what had gone down.

"Why didn't the Donahues go to the FBI?" he asked. "Go through the State Department? Maybe this whole thing could've been avoided."

"You don't need me to answer those questions." Reuben shifted on the hotel bed causing it to squeak beneath his weight. "If the Donahues contacted the police or FBI, the kidnappers threatened to kill their son. And let's just say they went ahead and contacted them anyway, you know it would take weeks to negotiate William's release, and that's only if they didn't kill him and dump his body somewhere first. The U.S. is focused on the embassy bombings and Al-Qaida, not some rich kid. Shoot, they're more interested in the president's affair with an intern."

"Maybe." Tom ran his hand across the day's growth along his jawline. "That still doesn't explain how your team operates. Who pays for all of this? Who ensures your safety?"

"We ensure our own safety. We've recruited and trained operatives and contractors from every branch of the military and government agency. We're small now, but we like it that way. Easier to maintain. Right now, Blackwater has the in with government contracts, so we're handling more private issues like the Donahue case, but the goal is that one day we'll have the connections that'll allow us to work some government operations too."

After tonight, Tom wasn't so sure that was a goal worth aiming for. "So the government funds Blackwater and the Donahues fund you."

"More or less." Reuben lifted a shoulder. "We have some investors too."

"And would those investors be satisfied that what happened tonight is normal?"

"No." Reuben's expression shifted, revealing that he, too, was affected by what happened to Kelly and O'Donnell. "Tonight wasn't ideal. But it happens. You know that better than anyone."

"Do they have families?"

"We all have families, Tom." Reuben answered sharply and then his expression softened. "They'll be taken care of."

Five words that didn't make him feel any better. He glanced through the doorway separating the adjoining room to where William Donahue sat curled against the headboard looking like anything but the partying college kid from the photos Mitchell had used to brief them on the flight to Ireland.

Money could buy a lot of things, but it couldn't take away the memories of what he'd just been through. Maybe William would do some good in his life—make the rescue that cost one man his life and left another in the balance worth it.

Was it worth it? They saved the kid and that was good, but they'd lost a man. Did the end justify the means?

Tom's attention shifted to Mitchell, who was on the phone talking to someone above Tom's paygrade about the next step of the mission to get William back to his family in the U.S. When that happened, would Reuben, Mitchell, and their counterparts in America consider it a success?

And what about Sean?

He'd failed that objective twice now. No wonder he was having trouble seeing this mission as anything but successful.

Reuben shifted, his weight causing the cheap floorboards beneath the thin carpet to creak. "Have you heard anything?"

Tom walked to the bedside table where his cell phone was plugged into the wall. Disappointment doubled down on him. "Nothing yet."

INITIUM

When they had arrived in Ireland, Tom had relied on old CIA assets and prayed they were far enough removed from current operations that it wouldn't expose Sean or endanger anyone else. It hadn't been easy, but he did manage to find a man whose cousin was a bartender for the same pub where members of the RIRA frequently met—including Sean. It was there his picture had been taken with two men involved in William's kidnapping.

William Donahue had looked at photos of Sean once they'd gotten to the hotel, but couldn't say one way or the other if he was one of the men who had grabbed him. He admitted that he'd been very drunk at the time. Tom was still having a hard time accepting the photos of Sean with the two kidnappers meant anything other than he was still alive.

A knock on the open door between the two hotel rooms drew their attention to Mitchell. "Gardaí made another arrest, one of the suspects from the money drop location. The fourth guy got away but they're hoping his friend will identify him."

Tom let out a slow breath. "Sean?"

"No." Mitchell shook his head, looking tired for the first time since Tom had met him. "We've secured a private flight out of Dublin at four."

Tom checked his watch. "That's in five hours." He looked at Reuben. "We can't leave until we find Sean."

"He's not our mission." Mitchell said, some of the fire returned to his gaze. "You knew what our objective was when we got here."

"We had a deal." Tom balled his fists. "You said if I identified the RIRA members and gave you locations, you'd allow me to find Sean."

"Negative." "I told you I'd give you an opportunity to identify Sean if he was present. He wasn't. We got the job done. Now we leave."

"You got the job done? At the cost of Kelly's life and maybe O'Donnell's? Who's going to answer for that?"

"Someone will, but it won't be us." Mitchell nodded to Reuben. "Wheels up at four, with or without him."

Mitchell backed into the adjoining room, sending a scathing look in Tom's direction before he stepped into the bathroom and slammed the door shut behind him.

Tom shook his head. "I can't leave without knowing about Sean."

Reuben pressed his lips together and stood. The metal coils of the cheap motel bed gave a loud squeak of gratitude. "I don't want to leave you behind, man."

"Then don't."

"That's not how it works."

Tom sighed, jet lag hitting him with a nauseating wave. "How does this work, exactly? One man's dead, another critically injured in a random shootout, and he's," Tom pointed at the closed bathroom door, "telling me you guys just walk away?"

"The Gardaí knows that Officer Kelly and O'Donnell were responding to a tip given to them about several members of RIRA who may have been involved in the Omagh bombing. That information led to the unfortunate incident that took place tonight outside of Belfast."

The mechanical tone in Reuben's voice chilled Tom. "Do you even hear yourself? Would a comment like that bring comfort to April and your kids if it was you instead of Kelly?"

Reuben's posture stiffened.

"I know Ireland wants to hold someone accountable for the Omagh bombing but the Gardaí and the government aren't just going to accept the story you've concocted. You don't think someone else knows about the kid?" Tom lowered his voice, glancing sideways at William in the other room. "I've worked here for five years. I know how these people work. Someone is going to put the truth together."

"Probably, but we won't be here when they do."

Tom shook his head. So easy to just walk away from the blowout—like the CIA did with Sean. He crossed the room to the window. He watched the twinkling lights of a city coming to life.

"Can we push back the flight? If I hear about Sean?"

Reuben's deep exhale gave him his answer.

"I can't leave until I know."

"You know what you're saying, right?" Reuben's voice was low. "No one knows you're here."

Tom glanced down at the city and tried to imagine leaving on a plane in five hours. He thought about Sam. The ring he had slid on her finger the day he asked her to marry him. In the privacy of that moment, her eyes sparkling with tears of joy, he made her a promise…

I will risk my heart for no one but you.

Sam probably believed that he meant he would love no other but her and that was true, but it meant more. Tom assured her he would do his job as an intelligence officer for the CIA to the best of his ability, but he would not seek out opportunity to risk his heart—his life—for anyone but Sam. It was why his decision to leave the agency hadn't been as difficult as he expected.

But now?

Would he be able to live with himself if he didn't at least try to find Sean? Not getting on that plane, staying in Ireland, meant he was breaking his vow to Sam. Would it be worth it?

CHAPTER EIGHT

2015
Washington, D.C.

TOM EDGED his car another two feet forward along I-295, eyeing the minivan and the numerous bumper stickers telling every driver what school, club, and team their child belonged to. He recognized the pride, but also the danger of such a display. He wasn't a parent, but he'd become an honorary one, watching Lyla grow up and enjoying major life moments without any of the angst most parents dealt with.

Lyla had been born with a rebellious streak—like wildfire, it was impossible to contain, much less predict the swiftly changing directions in likes, dislikes, mood, style, even hobbies.

When Lyla was thirteen, she'd quit ballet, tennis, and piano to join Babydoll Smashers, the local U15 roller derby team. Keith and Catherine were beside themselves fearing for her safety, but after Lyla's first round on the pitch that overturned the other team's jammer, she'd earned the nickname Stinkerbell, as well as her parent's support. Keith had even custom ordered sparkling green skates to match the wings Catherine found for Lyla to wear.

Tom chuckled at the memory of watching Lyla's opponents misjudge her small, fairy-like frame only to end up on their backsides when she revealed her strength. Or maybe it was the deep-set aggression?

Jack still hadn't called back with news about the vehicle Lyla got into outside of her family home. He'd told Keith to call him if they heard from Lyla and the fact that his cellphone remained quiet was not just unsettling—it was beginning to terrify him.

He dialed Jack's number.

"Hey boss. I've got someone at the Bureau working on pulling information on the vehicle, but he's not sure when he can get it back to us."

Tom slammed his palm against the steering wheel, frustration climbing. This wouldn't be an issue if they had someone in-house to handle their cyber needs. Another reminder that there was still more to do in the hiring department if he wanted his agency to operate successfully.

But it would all mean nothing if he didn't find Lyla.

"Did you ask him to pull information on Senator Donaldson?"

Jack hesitated. "Sir, you know the FBI will want more of a reason."

"How about his extra-marital activities." Tom ground his molars. "I don't think the Senate Ethics committee will look too kindly on one of their members being seen with an escort younger than his daughter."

"No, but we don't have proof." Mechanical ringing muted Jack's voice. "Hold on, boss, this might be the call we're waiting for."

Tom finally made it off the highway, but the traffic was just as congested on the frontage road. He drummed his fingers on the steering wheel waiting for Jack to come back on the line. When he did, it wasn't with the news he'd been expecting.

"Sir, the FBI just busted a prostitution ring ten minutes ago." Jack's voice came through the speaker. "They received a tip and obtained a search warrant. I'm guessing it's the same place Lyla's friend worked."

Tension coiled around Tom's gut. "What's that got to do with Lyla?"

"Uh, sir." The hesitation in Jack's voice warned Tom what was coming next. "Lyla was one of the girls taken into custody."

TWENTY MINUTES LATER, Tom pulled in front of the Third District police station in central D.C. His pulse picked up at the sight of a half dozen news vans lined up along Indiana Avenue and reporters lit up in front of cameras, spotlighting their version of the headline-making story.

It had taken some convincing to keep Keith at home with Catherine. Seeing this mess made Tom thankful he'd insisted.

"Boss," Jack met Tom inside the entrance where the cacophony of the media circus outside dropped off to the steady buzz of law enforcement activity inside. "They've just finished processing her and are holding her in the back. They're sending an officer to take you to her."

As Jack spoke, a young Black officer rounded the corner, her booted feet barely making a sound on the scuffed tile. Her dark eyes moved from Jack to Tom before lighting up. "Mr. Walsh, I didn't expect to see you here."

"Officer Jones, oh wait," Tom leaned forward, checking out the bars on her collar. "Captain Jones. Congratulations."

INITIUM

"Thank you, Mr. Walsh." Her smile stretched wide across her face. "You're with him?"

She tipped her head towards Jack and Tom nodded.

"Yes."

Captain Jones reached across the counter and pulled over a clipboard for Tom to sign his name on the visitor list. Setting the clipboard back, she waved her hand at someone sitting behind a bullet proof glass. A beep echoed from the door and Captain Jones escorted them toward the jail's holding cells.

Ahead of them, a handcuffed man was sitting on a bench, screaming obscenities. He looked over at them and got louder. The paternal part of Tom hated that Lyla had to hear the vulgar language echoing around them. Turning left, they walked down the hallway to the women's cells.

To their right was a large holding cell. Inside, a trio of young women huddled together. Lyla wasn't among them but, based off their fancy clothing, Tom would've guessed they were supposed to be out enjoying dinner at a steakhouse instead of standing in a ten-by-ten cement room that smelled of alcohol, urine, and cheap perfume.

"Ugh." Jack pressed his knuckles to his lips. "I don't know why, but for some reason I thought the women's section would be nicer."

"It's a jail, Jack." Tom looked over his shoulder. "What did you expect it to look like?"

"I don't know." Jack coughed. "But I didn't expect it to smell like a frat house."

On cue, a woman with bleached hair and tattoos barfed, causing the three fancy women to press themselves into the opposite corner.

"If being clocked in the head by my mama's shoes wasn't enough to keep me out of jail." Jack cringed. "That would've been."

Captain Jones rolled her head back with a sigh and then radioed for maintenance. She pointed at the third door on the left. "Ms. Fox is in room three."

"Your mom's shoes?" Tom asked as they continued down the hall.

Jack smiled, looking sheepish. "My mama's Italian and has an arm like Roger Clemens."

Tom chuckled and shook his head. He reached for the handle and paused when he heard Lyla's laughter coming from inside the room. Tom felt a jolt of shock. He wasn't sure how he'd expected to find Lyla, but laughing like she'd just heard the best joke wasn't it. He opened the door and stepped into interrogation room 3. Nor did he expect to find her flirtatiously smiling at a man whose suit coat was draped over her shoulders.

Tom gave her a quick once-over, making sure she was okay. Her long brown hair was wrapped up in a twist on the top of her head revealing a bright streak of blue that matched equally vibrant eye makeup, which in turn matched the high heels she'd paired with a black romper. Tom was certain she hadn't worn that to her parent's for dinner.

Lyla sat forward, smile disappearing.

"Tom."

The short clip of surprise was a far cry from the admiration she usually used when she saw him; like he was the favorite uncle. Her tone brought the young man sitting across from her to his feet, posture stiff. He eyed Tom with an appropriate amount of suspicion.

"I'm FBI Agent Devlin, and you are?"

Jack snorted behind Tom. "Thomas Walsh, here to take custody of Ms. Fox."

Agent Devlin frowned. "Custody? She's not in custody."

"She's not?"

"Don't sound so surprised." Lyla cocked an eyebrow at Tom

and then shrugged out of the suitcoat, handing it to Agent Devlin. "You have my number."

The tables turned. Now it was Tom eying the agent—whose cheeks were bright red—with suspicion. Taking his jacket, Devlin gave a nod to Tom, mumbling something about it being nice to meet him, then walked out the door.

"I've seen you before." Lyla's eyes narrowed on Jack. "You're the one who's been following me, or were you following that creep, Carter?" She faced Tom. "Please tell me you've been investigating that flea bag senator and his crony."

The glee in Lyla's voice was humorous but, given where they were sitting, he didn't think Keith or Catherine would think this was a laughing matter.

"You knew about Carter?"

Lyla's green eyes landed on Jack with an *are you serious* look. "The median age of residents in my apartment complex is seventy-five. Retired. Bored. Carter shows up and I've got every Mabel, Louise, and Ruth-Ann calling me to find out if I've got a new boyfriend."

Jack laughed, but Lyla shot him a look that made him cover it up with a cough.

"And in case *you* didn't notice," she added, "that black smoke coming out of your car means you need to take it into the shop. Or find another car. You might as well wave a flag announcing your location."

Before Jack could comment, Tom asked him. "Would you go meet with District Commander Landell? Let him know I'm here and will stop by to clear things up after I speak with Ms. Fox."

"Yes sir." Jack left, but not before a parting comment aimed at Lyla. "Who uses the word crony anymore?"

Lyla folded her arms and leaned back in her chair after the door closed behind Jack. "Did my dad send you?"

Tom took the seat Devlin had been in. "Tell me what happened."

"There's a police report."

"Lyla."

"It's on the news." She pointed through the window to a television mounted on the wall. She was right, the local news stations were playing video of federal and local law enforcement working a scene outside of a business called Lynx Ltd. Rolling footage showed a few young women like the ones he'd seen in the holding cell being led away along with a couple of older men.

"I want your version," he said, turning back to her.

"I was helping a friend." Lyla twisted her lips to the side. "Her parents don't have a lot of money and the scholarship she thought she was getting fell through, so she joined this escort business to hang out with men for a little extra money. She swore to me that it was just that. Nothing funny, like you know—" she wrinkled her nose. "Anyway, this senator got a little handsy and well, she got herself into a pickle and I just wanted to help her out."

Tom tilted his head to the news. "Looks like you did more than that."

Lyla's green eyes widened. "I didn't do that."

Tom frowned. "You didn't report the company?"

"No." She shook her head. "Cassidy called and said she got a call. That creepy senator had hired her for the night, and I wanted to get a picture of him..." She glanced up looking bashful.

"Were you planning on blackmailing a U.S. Senator, Lyla?"

"No." Lyla scooted forward on her chair. "I was just going to *suggest* it to Carter to get him to leave Cassidy alone."

Tom ran a hand down the back of his neck. Lyla had always been a helper, defender of the innocent, so her actions didn't surprise him. But she was in more than a pickle now. Senator Donaldson's connection to the Chicago Syndicate came through financial contributions that were no doubt given with strings attached. That could be deadly for anyone who got in the way—including a college girl trying to defend her friend.

"Look," he said. "I know you were trying to help. And that's good. But you have a great future ahead of you, Lyla."

"What future? The one my parents think I want?"

"There's nothing wrong with the life your parents want for you. They want you to be happy and successful."

Lyla pushed out a frustrated breath as if sitting here with him was a favor. "If they really wanted that for me then they'd listen to me."

"What do you mean?"

She fidgeted in her chair, tucking one leg under the other and then untucking it while retucking her long hair into a ball at the back of her head. After a moment, she blew out a breath and he could read the nervousness all over her face.

"What is it, Lyla?"

"I'm failing."

"Failing?"

"Physics." Lyla tipped her chin down.

Tom chuckled, relieved. "That's all? I was afraid you were going to tell me—"

"Literature." She lifted her head and locked eyes with him. "And marketing."

Now it was Tom's turn to fidget. He cleared his throat, "Okay, well, um—"

"Finance too."

He opened his mouth. Closed it. Opened it again, but he had no idea what to say.

Lyla's face crumpled, head flopping backwards against the chair. "My dad is going to kill me."

Tom shook his head. "No, he won't. He'll be disappointed but—"

An exaggerated moan of despair from Lyla cut him off. "That's worse." Tears gathered at the edge of her dark lashes and Tom's heart clenched.

"All I want to do is make them proud of me but, *ughhh*, I hate school. The stuffy professors, the mundane get up, go to class, study, write papers, football—well, I like the football games, but the whole thing feels so trivial when there are real world issues happening."

Her gaze challenged him. "Do you know what that Illinois Senator was asking my friend to do?"

He could imagine but preferred not to. "Lyla, I can take care of Senator—"

"You won't need to."

Tom's stomach twisted into a knot. "What do you mean?"

"Don't worry. Nothing illegal."

"Lyla."

"All I'm saying is that..." the corner of her lip tipped up a little. "I'm quitting school."

"You're what?"

"Quitting school."

Tom didn't know what it felt like to be a dad, but he was pretty sure his reaction to Lyla's declaration was spot on. "You cannot quit school, Lyla."

"It's too late." Her tone sounded resigned rather than angry. "Because of my low GPA, my advisor told me this is my last semester at Preston."

"I'm sure your Dad can make some calls and figure—"

"No." Lyla stood. "My dad isn't going to do anything because I don't want him to. Sitting in class is not where I belong."

She gestured to a cop that passed by. "I want to do more

INITIUM

with my life, help people. I can't explain it but deep down, I know it's what I'm supposed to do."

"What about finishing college first?"

She shook her head. "I'm not wasting my Dad's money or my time."

A familiar look came over her face and Tom prepared himself, knowing in the past it was just this look that had him buying Lyla a 1970 Chevelle. She'd fixed up the old car with the help of her high school mechanics class and then put it up for auction, targeting a financier who'd been looking for the car of his teenage dreams. Using her wealthy friends to drive up the bid, she got her target to give a final bid of close to half a million. Which she'd promptly donated to fund an arts program for five inner-city elementary schools.

Lyla seemed reckless at times, but she always had a plan.

"I figure I have two options." She moved her hand around the room. "I can work here with DC's finest. Or..."

That look.

"I can work for you, where you can nurture and guide me—protect me," she smiled. "And where I," she tipped her head to the television, "can bring some of my skills to the agency."

Tom twisted around and watched a *special news report* on the screen. Senator Craig Donaldson was being escorted from his home by two FBI Agents. Tom squinted. Was that Agent Devlin? He faced Lyla.

"One of my classmate's dad works for the Federal Election Commission." She shrugged. "They checked into a few things for me. The country might not know Senator Donaldson is a creepy cheater, but they'll know he's a liar and thief."

Looking back at the report, the ticker at the bottom read, *charges of campaign fraud, pilfering campaign contributions.* The Chicago Syndicate wasn't going to be pleased about that.

"So? Can I work for your new agency or should I stop by

Commander Landell's office before we leave? Ask him if rookies always start their careers working Barker Terrace."

Barker Terrace was one of the most dangerous neighborhoods in D.C., with violent crimes hovering at eighty percent. It was the last place he'd want to send any officer, much less Lyla. Employing her probably wasn't going to go over well with her parents, but he'd at least be able to keep an eye on the twenty-one year old—maybe keep her out of trouble and get her the training she'd need.

Lyla smiled her sweet smile, as if knowing she'd already won. Tom groaned and stood up.

"Come on, let's go break it to your parents."

CHAPTER NINE

AUGUST 31, 1998
Dublin, Ireland

TOM PAUSED OUTSIDE OF ST. Anne's cathedral, wishing it were open. Under the moon's glow, the Gothic architecture felt intimidating and yet it seemed to beckon him into its refuge offering a peace he wouldn't find anywhere else.

Beneath the centuries-old naves, would he find answers too?

What had he given up by remaining in Ireland?

It had been six days since the team left and Tom still didn't know where Sean was. The informant he'd spoken to a week ago said he'd seen someone looking like Connor Murphy meeting with members of the RIRA at a local pub in Belfast. It was a risk heading back to Belfast with the Gardaí still investigating the shootout but Tom had to know.

Tom had hit more than a dozen pubs and still no sign of Sean. Or the RIRA for that matter. So, he returned to Dublin wondering if someone had tipped them off? Had his informant been mistaken? Had God really given him a second chance to come back to Ireland, or was this just some attempt to assuage his guilt for leaving in the first place? And what if he didn't find Sean?

Two weeks. That's the promise he'd made to Sam when he called her a week ago telling her he was staying. Reuben expressed his concern about Tom digging into the RIRA without any backup, but Tom couldn't just walk away a second time without doing everything he could to try and find Sean. That had been enough for Sam.

But now? Could he leave in a week without any answers?

What if what Jennings said was true?

It was that question that kept him reaching out to old sources, pushing quietly for any information on Connor Murphy. If Sean was alive, it was because of his alias, and Tom had to be careful. He couldn't risk exposing him or any mission that might endanger another intelligence officer's life.

The guilt of Kelly's death hung over Tom like a dark cloud. O'Donnell had survived, but the bullet that struck his spine ended his career in the Gardaí. Both men were raw reminders of what was at stake.

Turning away from the sleeping church, Tom shoved his hands into his pockets and headed back to the motel. A wave of homesickness hit him, and he longed to hear Sam's voice. He thought about the satellite phone Reuben insisted on leaving with him. His friend couldn't promise immediate help but if a call was made, if Tom was in trouble, then at least someone would know.

Samantha wouldn't be left wondering.

Tom picked up his pace, anxious to get back to the motel and call her. Even just imagining the sound of her voice energized him. He was unlocking his motel room door when a shrill

INITIUM

ringing echoed from his pocket. Stepping into his room, Tom pulled the mobile phone out and answered.

"Hello?"

"The Red Hall. One hour."

Toms' pulse pounded. "Excuse me?" But no one answered. "Hello?"

The line went dead. Tom pulled the phone away from his ear and stared down at it trying to place the voice. It wasn't familiar and it didn't sound like Tyrone, his informant. *Red Hall. One hour.* He checked his watch. Fifteen past ten. The pubs in Belfast were likely beginning to grow busy. In an hour they'd be bustling with the last of the tourists mingling with locals on a Friday night.

Slipping the phone back into his pocket, he walked to the dresser and grabbed the old newsboy cap Sean used to tease him about. If that phone call meant Sean was going to be at Red Hall, then it would offer him an inconspicuous way to know Tom was there. If the call meant something else....

His eyes flickered to the motel safe. Reuben had left one more thing besides the satellite phone. The P226. The key to the safe was tucked into the bottom of his shoe inside the closet. Taking the gun somehow felt like he was inviting trouble, but so was walking into a situation blind.

Tom thought about Sam and the phone call that wouldn't happen now. His chest ached as he grabbed his room key and walked out of his motel, leaving the gun and praying that whatever happened tonight meant he would be on his way back to her soon.

THE RED HALL was a pub identified among dozens lining South Great George's Street by its red and white striped awning. The Victorian-style bar was ornately decorated to match its name. A faded red and gold carpet muted the noise of the room, and the bright red ceiling was painted to match the leather barstools lining the long mahogany bar top running the length of the building on both sides.

Tom stepped into the din of regulars and locals sharing stories over their glasses of whiskey and beer. He searched faces and profiles of those inside for Sean, but had no luck. Frustration and desperation warred in his stomach. He checked the time. He was early, but only by a few minutes. *Relax.*

The bartender eyed him, warning Tom that he was beginning to stick out. You didn't walk into a pub and not order a drink. He pulled out some money and placed it on the bar.

"Tullamore Dew, straight."

The man gave a nod and set down the glass he was cleaning with a towel before grabbing a bottle of the Irish whiskey. With his glass in hand, Thomas found a stool next to a couple where he could keep an eye on who was coming in or going out.

TWO HOURS LATER, Tom pushed aside his drink and the local paper, having read it front to back—twice. To keep up appearances he'd allowed the liquor to touch his lips a few times, which left the glass full. Thankfully, most inside the Red Hall were too busy to take notice. Or so he'd thought.

"Something wrong with your drink?"

Tom glanced up into the russet-colored eyes of a female bartender with fiery red hair that reached her waist. He'd caught her looking his way a couple of times throughout the night.

"No, no. I'm just not in the mood I guess."

She dropped her towel on his table and wiped, leaning low. Eyes meeting his, she whispered, "You best call it a night then, lest you grab the wrong kind of attention."

INITIUM

He must've looked confused because she tipped her head to a group of men gathered at one end of the bar. Tom had noticed a couple of them come in earlier, but they sat separately so he didn't think anything of it. But now....

He stopped the bartender as she reached for the glass. "I'll stay, thanks."

"We're closed." She shook his hand off and took his glass. "Find yourself a new place."

Tom would've protested had it not been for the curious look of the man sitting to his left. Taking her not so subtle hint, Tom rose from his stool and pulled out some coins, which he dropped into the tip jar at the counter.

A man stepped backwards in front of Tom, colliding with his shoulder.

"Oi, mate," came the gruff voice. "Watch yourself."

"Sorry." Tom held up his hands, but when his eyes met the ones staring down on him he stopped cold.

Sean.

Or at least it looked like Sean. Except for the rough beard and dull, sunken eyes that looked like a death mask in the dim light of the bar. Like they'd been aged with grief.

"I'm sorry." Tom took a step back if only to give himself a better look, but the man turned on his heel to face the row of men watching. He leaned in, hands on their shoulders as he spoke to them, ignoring Tom as he stood there.

One of the men glanced back. "You got a problem?"

The Irish brogue was harsh and matched the glint in his eyes. Sean, if it was him, didn't look back.

"He was just leavin'." The redheaded bartender spoke for him. "Right?"

Tom nodded in her direction. "Yes."

He tried to move around the group, but the man he

believed to be Sean straightened and backed into Tom hard enough he stumbled sideways.

"Seems you got a problem, lad." The glinty-eyed one snarled.

Before Tom could respond, the bearded man grabbed the collar of his leather coat and dragged him towards the exit without a word. Outside, the brisk air smacked him in the face almost as hard as he was shoved forward.

A few locals paused to watch.

"This pub ain't for tourists. Find your pint elsewhere."

Tom frowned and turned to face the man, straightening his shoulders. He narrowed his eyes, slightly worried it would be taken as a threat, but he needed to know.

"Connor?"

The man's eyes grew tight as slits. "What did you call me?"

Tom swallowed. "Are you Connor Murphy?"

In two quick strides the man's hands were fisted around Tom's collar again, his breath hot on his face.

"I told you to find another pub, mate. Leave. Don't ever come back."

With a hard shove that nearly put Tom on his backside, the man spit, turned and went back into Red Hall. The small crowd dispersed, voicing their disappointment with jeers and laughter at Tom's expense. He stood, straightening his coat and feeling the sting of anger and frustration.

Tom walked away, careful not to look back at the pub, trying to make sense of what had happened. Trying to reconcile the Sean he knew with the man he'd just seen. Taking cover in the shadows of an alley he paused and listened. No one was following him.

He checked his watch, let out a sigh, and settled his back against the cold brick. Most pubs would begin shutting down around two, and he hoped that meant the man who looked like

INITIUM

Sean would be exiting soon. Unless, as it sometimes happened, Red Hall decided to extend its hours for special guests. Tom pulled out a piece of gum and popped it into his mouth. Then settled in to wait out the night.

Because he believed, without a doubt, he'd found Sean.

CHAPTER TEN

SEPTEMBER 1, 1998
Dublin, Ireland

A SNORT of laughter jolted Tom out of his doze. He shook away the heaviness of sleep and edged toward the corner of the building. Across the street, a trio of men stood on the stoop of Red Hall. The lights of the pub were dimmed low, forcing Tom to squint to get a good look at their faces.

There had been at least four or five men inside the pub, but now just three remained. Panic washed through him. Two minutes. He'd closed his eyes for two minutes. Had he missed Sean?

The men parted, each going a different direction. *Great.* Tom stepped out further, not caring that he risked being seen. He immediately dismissed the man heading left—too short to be Sean.

The second man, heading right, passed beneath a street lamp. Beard, about Sean's height and build. Tom glanced at the

INITIUM

third guy. Same. The initial shock of seeing Sean, if it was him, had kept Tom from paying attention to the clothing. Fifty-fifty shot, but if he was wrong, he risked losing Sean again.

Lord, let me pick the right one.

Before meeting Sam, Tom would've thought it ridiculous to pray for such a trivial thing. But now he could hear her reminding him that it was easy to trust God with the big things but trusting Him with the little things meant we recognized our need and His sovereignty.

Tom waited just long enough for man number two to disappear around a corner before starting after man three for no other reason than he chose a walkway that cut through Stephen Street, giving Tom plenty of places to duck into if necessary.

Keeping his distance, Tom studied the man ahead of him. He had a bit of a limp which Tom didn't remember Sean having. Doubt crept in. Was he following the wrong guy? The man cut left, bypassing Dubh Linn Garden, and dropped down a set of stairs that led to Castle Street. The eight-foot stone walls on either side wouldn't give Tom any cover but he had no choice.

Tom waited at the top of the stairwell for a minute, allowing the man to get a good start ahead of him. He had a moment of panic after his foot hit the bottom step and he didn't immediately see the man, but then a darkened silhouette appeared about ten or twelve yards ahead.

Tom sped up his pace as they approached Castle Street. There wasn't a lot of traffic at this time of night but there were many avenues the man could disappear down or, worse, he could grab a taxi.

The man rounded the corner, heading right and out of sight. Tom broke into a jog and had barely stepped onto the street when a fist flew at his face, connecting with his jaw, and causing his head to snap back. Tom tried to regain his balance, but strong hands shoved him backwards, slamming him into a wall.

"Why're ya following me, mate?"

Tom peered back at the man, but a streetlight overhead cast his face in deep shadows making it impossible to know for sure if it was Sean. Tom massaged his jaw, it wasn't broken but he sure felt like the man had bricks for fists. "I, uh, wasn't. I'm going to my motel."

"*Bréagadóir.*" The man spat and turned on his heel.

"I'm not a liar."

The man rounded again, and Tom forced himself not to flinch. "Then yer' looking for trouble."

"I'm looking for my friend. Connor Murphy."

If this man was Sean, there was no visible response to Tom saying his name. But that wasn't what bothered him. If this man *wasn't* Sean, but a member of the RIRA—there should've been a reaction. Before the bombing, the name Connor Murphy would have caused a stir. He'd gained quite a reputation within the organization, which this man would've known were he RIRA. It was odd...unless, if this was Sean and he was still playing a part, living out his alias.

Looking around, most of the apartments were dark. No signs of anyone watching them but he couldn't be sure. Someone had tipped off Tom to the bar and that led to Sean—or a man that looked like him—but if this *was* him, why wasn't he breaking cover when it was clear they were alone? Was it possible Sean was upset they'd left him? Or was his anger because of Annie?

Tom took a small step towards the man. "Connor?"

A throaty sound of irritation was the only answer. The man turned on his heel and Tom took another step. His jaw ached and he was exhausted, but the questions ended here. Tonight. It was a huge risk, but he had to know.

INITIUM

"I'm sorry about Annie."

All Tom saw was a wall of knuckles flash in front of his face before he hit the ground. The back of his head smacked hard on the concrete, but it was the horrendous pain in his nose that had him moaning. He squeezed his watering eyes closed, grinding his teeth as if that would somehow help with the pain. *He got his response.* Wait. Did that mean—

Tom opened his eyes. Twisting to his side, he searched the street. Empty. He rolled to his knees and pushed himself to his feet feeling a bit lightheaded. Wobbling, he leaned his head forward and watched the dripping blood pool into a puddle at his feet. He tried wiping at his nose but cringed the second his fingers brushed against the skin.

Taking a careful breath, Tom gave himself a second allowing his head to clear before he staggered toward his motel. His frustration throbbed with the pain in his nose. He pressed the back of his hand as gently as he could against his nose in a weak attempt to stop the blood still dripping down his chin.

"What did you do to yerself?"

To his right the redhead from the bar crossed the street walking towards him. "I didn't do this to myself."

The redhead dug through her bag and pulled out a long scarf. She balled it up and handed it to him. "Press this against yer nose."

A soft perfume scent wafted from the floral fabric and Sam popped to mind. Tom shook his head. "I wouldn't want to ruin it."

She eyed him skeptically. "So you're just going to bleed all over the street instead?"

Tom pressed the hem of his jacket near his nose and winced. "Maybe."

"Hold still." Moving closer, the woman put her hand at the back of his head, her fingers cool against his neck. She took the scarf and gently wiped it against his cheek, jaw, and above his lip. "It doesn't look broken, but you should probably see a medic. There's a twenty-four-hour place around—"

"I'll be fine." Tom said, leaning out of her touch. "I just need to get back to my motel room."

The redhead stood, holding out her scarf to him. "Walking around with blood smeared across your face is a surefire way to draw unwanted attention. Dublin is beautiful but like most big cities we're not immune from predators taking advantage of wounded prey. Especially of the American variety."

"My motel isn't far." He pointed to O'Lucky's Motel. "See."

"Well, let me walk you there. Make sure you get to your room without further incident."

Tom swallowed. He'd chosen O'Lucky's because he could pay cash and didn't need to give his ID for a room. It didn't take him long to realize the motel had a reputation for its hourly rates.

"I'm engaged." Tom blurted out.

Her eyes widened, confused, and then she laughed. A strong and bubbly noise that echoed loudly against the quiet of the night and rankled his nerves.

"What?" he asked.

"I'm just tryin to help ya, not date ya."

Embarrassment set his cheeks on fire. "I'm sorry, I didn't mean to presume—"

"Come on, lad." She moved her hands in a herding motion toward O'Lucky's. She pointed to a multistory stone building with a turquoise door a few buildings down from the hotel. "That's my place and I promise I won't try to put the moves on ya."

Not wanting to cause a scene in the middle of the street, especially because his nose was still dripping blood, Tom let the

INITIUM

redhead lead him to his motel room. He went to pull his key from his pocket, but she stopped him.

"You didn't leave your door open did ya?" She asked. Her voice low.

"No."

"Didn't think so."

The door was ajar. Stepping in front of the woman, he kicked it the rest of the way open, body tense and ready to fight. He wouldn't be taken by surprise this time. The room was ransacked.

"I think you should come to my place."

"I'm going to call the Gardaí and—"

The redhead put her hand on his arm, the touch causing him to look back at her. "If yer lookin' for information about yer friend, you need to come with me now."

Tom frowned at the way her tone had gone from friendly barkeep to someone who was used to giving orders. "Who are you?" he asked, wishing again he'd thought to bring his gun.

"Really?"

"Sophie Bridges, London counter-intelligence."

CHAPTER ELEVEN

SEPTEMBER 1, 1998
Dublin, Ireland

TOM NEEDED ANSWERS. Was it only a few hours ago he'd been standing in front of St. Patrick's thinking the same thing? Now he had more questions than answers. He removed another cotton ball from his nostril, less blood on it than earlier, and dropped it into the wicker trash basket with the others.

He glanced at the bathroom door, the only private space in the tiny apartment Ms. Bridges had walked them to. *Private space* was generous. He didn't have to guess what she was doing behind the door, the sound of the shower as loud as if he was in the shower himself.

A spring from the couch poked into his thigh like a prick to his conscience. He jumped off the couch, wanting to pace but not having anywhere to do so. Tom needed to call Sam—to hear her voice—but whoever ransacked his motel room didn't just take the gun, they'd taken his satellite phone too.

INITIUM

"I'm MI5."

Tom wasn't sure if it was the shock of that statement mixed with the pain in his nose, but he ignored years of training that warned him trusting the redhead could be dangerous. The running water shut off. If she was going to kill him, he didn't think she'd clean up before the deed was done.

He scanned the sparsely furnished apartment. Besides the couch, there was a worn table and two mismatching chairs next to a counter with a sink, single burner stove, and small oven. If this was a safehouse, surely there'd be a satellite phone somewhere that he could use to let Sam know where he was.

The door opened and Ms. Bridges stepped out in a cloud of steam, wearing sweatpants and a thermal shirt. She towel-dried her hair and tipped her head toward the bathroom. "Shower's all yers. I can probably find a shirt that'll fit ya, but I've got nothing for your lower half."

Tom swallowed. "I, uh, I'll pass."

She paused, narrowed her eyes on him. "You some kind of saint or something?"

That sounded like an insult. "No. I'm just—"

"Engaged." She smiled. "You mentioned that."

Tom noticed the subtle shift in her Irish accent as it melted away, revealing her British heritage. "You wouldn't happen to have a satellite phone, Ms. Bridges?"

Dropping the towel on the back of one of the spindled chairs, she picked up a kettle and filled it with water. "The name is Sophie and I don't know what the rules are for American agents, but British agents can't be making personal calls on their SATs."

Tom's breath stalled in his chest. "What makes you think I'm an agent?"

"Do ya think I'd really expose myself if I didn't know ya

were CIA?" She took a mug off a peg and dropped a teabag inside.

"Two nights ago, another MI5 agent spotted ya outside a local hangout for RIRA members. Ran your photo through our system and our director immediately gets a call from someone named Jennings. Tea?"

Tea? Tom blinked up at her waiting expression and shook his head. Tea was the last thing on his mind after being told Jennings not only knew he was in Ireland, but had told an MI5 officer that he was a former intel officer for the CIA.

"I don't know what the rules are for MI5, but in the CIA, we don't blow our cover unless there's a reason." He moved her damp towel to the rack inside the bathroom and returned to the chair to sit. "So why am I here, Ms. *Bridges*?"

"Sophie. It *is* my name." Her Irish brogue slipped in. Carrying her tea to the table, she sat. "Why'd ya leave?"

"Leave?"

"The Agency."

So, Jennings didn't tell them everything. "Let's call it irreconcilable differences."

She seemed to consider his answer for a moment before taking another sip of tea. "I've been given authorization to share information with ya on the agreement that ya return the favor."

Authorization? When had she—his eyes moved to the bathroom. *The bathroom.* Tom checked out her wet hair...had she actually showered or was that just a ruse to keep him off balance?

"Are we in agreement?"

Tom met her eyes. "I don't know what favor you expect from me. You know I'm no longer with the agency."

"How did ya know about tonight?"

Tom frowned. "What do you mean?"

"That group hasn't been into the pub in weeks and on the

INITIUM

same night they come back—ya show up in all your American glory."

"The subtlety of your insults is impressive, but I'd expect MI5 would spend more effort training their officers to maintain their accent."

Ms. Bridges smirked and reached across the table for a napkin before passing it to him. "Your nose is bleeding again."

Without thinking he pressed the napkin to his nose, sharp pain reminding him to be gentle.

"Why don't we talk about the man who did that to ya."

He stared at her through watering eyes. Tom had no idea how much Jennings told her or her superiors, but he wouldn't be the one to oust Sean. "He's got a good right hook."

She sipped her tea, her eyes moving to his chest. "Seemed *personal*."

Tom looked down at the bloody stain on his shirt. *I'm sorry about Annie*. Ms. Bridges was right—it was personal. Those four words nearly earned him a broken nose, but it was worth it. He was more certain than ever the bearded man he'd followed tonight was Sean. What he wasn't certain about was why Ms. Bridges was interested in him.

"You said something about sharing information with me?"

Ms. Bridges smiled and Tom noted that it was a nice one.

"Very well. We know your Agency had been operating in Omagh the last several years, monitoring the Real IRA, same as us. The morning of August fifteenth our intel picked up information about a vehicle carrying a bomb into Omagh. But someone prevented that intel from reaching the Royal Ulster Constabulary, which..." her expression turned somber. "Well, you know what happened."

Tom did and it didn't make the pain in his chest hurt any less, especially when he thought of Annie and her baby. If it had been Sam…the pain in his nose suddenly felt insignificant compared to what Sean must be feeling.

"The Irish government wants answers, Mr. Walsh. And we intend to help them find out who was responsible and make them pay."

There was an element of revenge in Ms. Bridges tone that made Tom uncomfortable.

"And you think the men at the pub tonight were behind the bombing?"

"One in particular. Connor Murphy."

Tom stiffened. There was no hesitation in her accusation. Just a simple statement that mirrored what Jennings suggested weeks ago. *Was* Sean involved?

"We know Connor Murphy is an operative imbedded in the RIRA, your Agency gave us that much. But what we don't know is why he's decided to turn traitor."

"He's not a traitor." Tom regretted the amount of emotion in his voice, giving him away.

Ms. Bridges arched her brow. "That's not what our reports are saying."

Tom needed to turn the tables. "Tell me."

"There's a photo of a father posing with his child next to a red Vauxhall Cavalier, the vehicle that carried the bomb into Omagh. The same vehicle Murphy was photographed driving two days before."

His breathing stilled.

"Two weeks ago," she continued. "Murphy was seen sharing drinks with the man currently in Gardaí custody for the shootout that happened outside of Belfast. Rumors are circling that man was connected to the kidnapping of an American college student."

Tom pressed his lips together, thinking about the photo Reuben produced with Sean and William Donahue and other

INITIUM

members of the RIRA. He studied Ms. Bridges. Did she know about Tom's involvement in the Donahue mission?

"If you have this information why haven't you alerted the Irish Gardai? Have them pull him in for questioning?"

Ms. Bridges blew out a breath, pushed her mug aside. "Because there's going to be another attack."

Tom sat straighter. "When?"

She shook her head. "We don't know, but we're hoping you can help us find out."

"How?"

"Answer my original question. How did you know to come to Red Hall tonight?"

"I received a phone call. The caller gave me the name of the bar and a time."

She narrowed her eyes on him. "The caller?"

"He didn't give me his name."

"Did you recognize his voice?"

"Not really."

"And yet you trusted this mystery caller enough to show up at the same bar as five ranking RIRA members?" She looked on him with disbelief. "Someone wanted you there tonight and I want to know why."

"I don't know." Tom answered honestly. "But I know Connor Murphy wasn't involved in Omagh or the kidnapping. He's not a traitor."

"That's not what the intel suggests."

A week's worth of exhaustion came down on him in that moment. "I don't care what the intel suggests. What man would allow a bomb to explode in the very location where his pregnant wife is shopping?"

Ms. Bridges stayed silent.

"Connor Murphy would never put their lives or anyone else's in danger. If he could've stopped it—he would've."

"Then you have a vested interest in helping us—proving your friend's innocence."

Sophie picked up her mug and stood. "You're no longer an employee of the CIA, Mr. Walsh. If what you believe is true and you want to help your friend then I'm offering you an opportunity to become an asset for MI5 and help us prevent another attack."

An asset for MI5? If that meant he'd have access to Sean and clearing his name, bringing him home....

"What do you need me to do?"

Ms. Bridges set her mug in the sink. "We've got an officer on the inside that's passed information the next attack will be another bomb, but they're waiting on the material to be delivered."

"Who's it being delivered to?"

"Connor Murphy." Sophie's words sent ice through Tom's veins. "Connor Murphy is building the bomb."

CHAPTER TWELVE

2016
Washington, D.C.

TOM CAUGHT Lyla's quick glances at the man sitting in his office. Maybe the modern glass and steel walls weren't a great idea. It offered no privacy, but it did allow him a panoramic view of the Capitol and a direct line of sight over the large open space of the SNAP Agency's inner hub where Jack and Lyla were currently working.

Or should be.

He met Lyla's gaze with a lift of his brow, and she quickly swiveled in her chair, turning her back to him. He briefly wondered if there'd ever be a day he didn't question his decision to hire her before letting out a breath and refocusing his attention on the young man who'd walked in ten minutes ago, looking for a job.

Young was relative. Nicolás Garcia was close in age to Jack, but he didn't even have to look at the man's file to know Nicolás had lived a lifetime of experiences. Tom could see it in the depths of his dark eyes.

"Tell me, Nicolás," he asked. "What makes you think you'd be a good fit for my agency?"

"If you don't mind, I prefer Garcia, sir." Nicolás Garcia shifted in his seat, his roughened fingers pawing at the worn Red Sox ballcap he'd placed on his knee. "And I'm not sure, sir. Truth is, I don't know much about your agency."

"Yet you want to work here?"

"No." Nicolás answered. "I want to work for you."

Tom leaned back in his chair, assessing Garcia's stiff posture, the set of his jaw, a piercing gaze that would make most bristle under their scrutiny. Was the answer he'd just given Tom flattery? Honesty? Or desperation?

Garcia didn't cower under the scrutiny; his military bearing at ease in the silence.

Tom glanced at Garcia's resume. It was succinct. Ten years in the Army. Special Forces Explosives Ordnance Disposal officer. But then, nothing.

"There's a gap between the time you left the military and now. Why?"

Garcia's shoulders tensed and the muscle in his jaw ticked. Subtle indicators, the only ones Tom noticed, to suggest a falter in the soldier's confidence. "I took a bit of time to reassess my goals."

Tom waited for him to continue but Garcia apparently was done explaining. *Interesting.* He set the paper down on a closed file. One containing all the information Garcia was withholding.

"With your background I would assume you'd be a desirable candidate for SWAT or Homeland Security."

Garcia maintained eye contact, but Tom could sense the battle warring behind them.

INITIUM

"I was hired by the Special Operations Division. Trained with them for a few months. It wasn't a good fit."

That much was true. With the help of a cyber tech Tom had sub-contracted, it hadn't taken longer than ten minutes to learn all about Garcia's temporary employment status with Metro SWAT. On paper, Garcia was overqualified for their current workload but that didn't mean in the future his experience wouldn't be beneficial.

Off paper, Garcia's Special Tactics team leader, Captain Ortega, spoke highly of his character. His Army Commander repeated much the same except....

"I know Captain Ortega, Mr. Garcia." Tom continued to study Garcia's stiff posture. "He believed you had great potential for his team. If there's a reason why it didn't work, I'd like to know why."

"If you've looked into my employment record then I have no doubt you've researched my military career as well." Garcia's shoulders relaxed and he lifted the ballcap off his knee as he stood. "I can't sit here and pretend you don't know more about me than I do about this agency. I came here because I owed it to Colonel DeAntona. He helped me out and I guess he thought maybe I'd be...well, anyway. I appreciate your time, sir."

"Why weren't you a good fit for SWAT, Garcia?"

Garcia paused at the door.

"Ego, sir. In the Army we have one goal, to protect life to the utmost. A few of my teammates in SWAT had other goals. Headlines. In my experience, humility never makes a headline. Pride goes before destruction."

"And a haughty spirit before a fall." Tom finished the old proverb.

Garcia clearly wasn't one to answer quickly, but his words held meaning. He was a rare breed.

Tom glanced across the vast office space to the area currently being set up for their own cyber tech. That was the position Tom needed to fill next—the position he had earmarked for the budget. He rose from his chair.

"Mr. Garcia, I appreciate you coming in, but I can't offer you a full-time position in the agency currently. However," he said, coming alongside Garcia and offering his hand. "If we accept an assignment where your skillset could be beneficial, I'd like to contract your services. Once our agency grows, maybe offer you a permanent position in the future."

"I appreciate that, sir." Garcia accepted the handshake. Tom watched as the young man passed Lyla's workstation and paused.

"Your diagram is wrong." Garcia said, pointing to the schematics of the old Attebury canning warehouse.

Tom smiled as Lyla bristled. "I'm sorry." Lyla snapped, "Who are you?"

"If you're trying to get into the building, there's no doorway there or there." Garcia tapped the drawing. "And the ductwork right here has been replaced to make room for a door over here."

"I've been surveilling that building for the last two weeks, I think I know the floorplan."

"You're wrong." Garcia shrugged. "Call the city. Ask them for blueprints prior to eighty-nine."

"I have all the blueprints."

"Not if that's your plan." Garcia tipped his head to Lyla and then walked past her. "Good luck."

"*Good luck.*" Lyla mimicked and Tom gave her a look. As if sensing his displeasure, she turned toward him. "What? I've been inside the building, there's not a door in the middle of the wall."

Garcia stopped and turned, a smirk the only thing coloring

INITIUM

his otherwise patient expression. He walked back to the whiteboard and tapped an area to the east of Lyla's sketch.

"Attebury was constructed in 1893, nearly twenty-five years before prohibition came to D.C. Over here is a restaurant, Izzy's, named after Isadore Einstein from New York. Do you know who he is?"

Lyla bit her lip, folded her arms over her chest. "Should I?"

"Maybe." Garcia looked back at Tom. "Isadore, *Izzy*, Einstein was a G-man. An FBI agent who busted speakeasies."

Picking up a marker, Garcia marked three x's on the board. "Guess the owner of Attebury thought it'd be funny to name his speakeasy after him. Employees of the cannery entered the speakeasy here and these two doors were for a fast escape."

"Did you request *all* the floorplans for the building, Lyla?" Jack asked.

"I..." She looked from Jack back to Garcia and back to Tom. "I, I'm not sure. I asked for everything they had, but maybe they just gave me the most current ones."

Garcia slipped his ballcap onto his head. "Attebury was abandoned for about forty years before D.C. began revitalizing the warehouse district a year ago. SWAT used to train there."

"You're SWAT."

"No." Tom answered for Garcia. "He's the newest member of our team." Meeting Garcia's surprised expression, he added. "Morning briefings begin at eight."

"Yes, sir." Garcia nodded. "Thank you, sir."

"Would you set Garcia up with an ID card for the building, Jack?" Tom asked, turning back to his office. "Lyla. A word."

"Sir," Lyla said as she followed him into his office. "How was I supposed to know the guy at the city plans office didn't give me the most current floorplans? I asked him for everything."

"That's the job, Lyla, we can't afford to make a mistake—"

"I understand, but I would've caught it." Lyla blew out a breath clearly frustrated before her gaze dipped downward. "I'm sorry, sir. It won't happen again."

A year in and Tom still wasn't used to Lyla calling him "sir." A year in and Lyla was still fighting to prove herself. She was young, but so far her age hadn't been a hinderance to their assignments. Her stubbornness, well, that was a different story.

"What'd you think of him?"

"Who?" She thumbed in the direction where Jack had walked Garcia out. "Him?"

"Yes."

She shrugged and began playing with the hem of her shirt. "I don't know. He seems a bit uptight."

Tom gathered the resume Garcia had given him and opened up the file he'd made earlier that day, adding it to the information he'd collected from his former commander.

"He comes with a wealth of experience." And regret that Tom sensed Garcia carried around like a hundred-pound ruck sack. "I think he'll be valuable to the Attebury assignment."

"What?" Lyla gawked. "Attebury is mine."

"Garcia's all set—"

"I make one little mistake and Mister Cowboy walks in with his worn jeans and boots like he's some kind of Tim McGraw."

"His name is Nicolás Garcia." Tom put the file into his desk. "And I'm not giving your assignment to him. You two are going to work together on Attebury."

She crossed her arms over her chest. "I'm still lead?"

"It doesn't always have to be a competition, Ly." Jack shook his head.

"I'm not competing," a coy smile filled her face. "But I get to be in charge, right? I'm still the lead."

Tom inhaled, meeting Jack's *what are you going to do now*

INITIUM

look through the glass. "Yes, Lyla. You're still the lead. But Garcia brings valuable experience to our team. I expect you'll allow him to do his job."

"Fine, fine." She waved her hand and started to leave.

"Wait, his name is Garcia?"

"Nicolás Garcia." Tom answered. "But he prefers to be called by his last name."

"*Nicolás.*" Lyla let his name roll of her lips. "*Nic-o-lás.*" She smiled. "This is going to be fun."

Tom watched Lyla go back to her workstation. She sat and spun in her chair and then picked up her phone, Tom hoped to call the city for an updated floorplan.

"Are you sure about this?" Jack asked, coming into Tom's office.

Tom sat down, removed his glasses, and rubbed the old scar on the bridge of his nose.

"No," he answered Jack. "But I have a feeling that if there's anyone who can keep Lyla in check, it's going to be Nicolás Garcia."

CHAPTER THIRTEEN

SEPTEMBER 1, 1998
Dublin, Ireland

TOM GLANCED through the Renault's windshield at the green telephone box where Ms. Bridges was on the phone with her contact inside of the Real IRA. Ms. Bridges had made only one stop before this one. An electronics store that should've been closed before seven on a Sunday morning, but for some reason had been opened to her. She'd returned with a mobile and a calling card.

"Are you safe?" Sam's voice crackled in Tom's ear.

There was enough sunlight peeking through the clouds to cast a reflection on the passenger window of his bruised face and busted nose.

"Yes."

Sam stayed quiet. Or maybe it was the lag? "You still there?"

"Do you have anyone there helping you?" Sam's voice felt

as distant as the thousands of miles that separated them. "Someone you can trust to help you find your friend?"

He looked back over at Ms. Bridges. Last night, she'd shown him the false door in the bathroom that opened to a secret room behind the tiny apartment. It held a bed, a desk and computer and was where she slept after offering him the couch until their early morning call. Did he trust her? What choice did he have?

"I think so, yes. Yes."

"I miss you." Tom read the undertone in Sam's soft statement. Without asking, she wanted to know if he was going to keep his promise.

"I hope to be home soon." He had one week left.

Ms. Bridges crossed the street, an urgency to her step and a deep frown on her face. "I need to go now but I promise I'll call as soon as I can."

"Stay safe."

Tom ended the call just as Ms. Bridges climbed in. "What's wrong?"

"They're gone."

"Who? Connor?"

"All of them. They must've gotten the material and now—" she jerked her head to him, eyes zeroing in on him. "They bolted because of you."

"I didn't do anything."

"Except show up." She hit the steering wheel with her hand. "Eejit."

Tom knew what that word meant. "Do you know where they could've gone?"

"Most likely the next target."

"Call your contact." He handed over the mobile phone he'd called Sam with. "If you've had officers monitoring Murphy, find out which locations he's visited multiple times."

Ms. Bridges hesitated and then dialed a number. Tom rubbed a thumb over the bruise along his cheek. Why had Sean reacted so strongly to him? Wouldn't he know Tom would keep him safe? Unless he wasn't. Maybe this was his fault—had his appearance last night set them off?

"We've got three locations." Ms. Bridges leaned across him, opened the glovebox, and pulled out a map of Dublin. Spreading it between them, she flipped the visor and caught the marker that dropped down. "Murphy's been moving around a lot but there are three locations he's returned to several times in the last week and a half."

She pointed to a spot on the map. "Cathal Brugha Barracks." Her finger jabbed another spot. "Pearce Street Gardaí Station and," she looked up. "Shackelton Barracks in Ballykelly."

Ballykelly was in Northern Ireland. "How long ago did they leave?"

Ms. Bridges checked her watch. "About an hour ago."

"Put Shackleton on alert. If Connor is headed there, they have two hours or so to prepare." Tom looked at Ms. Bridges. "Do you have a contact at the Gardaí?"

"Yes."

"Call them and let them know there's an imminent threat against their station and to be prepared."

"I'm not certain you're the one to be giving me orders."

"Okay." Tom said. "What do you want to do?"

Ms. Bridges looked down at the map and then back up at him. "You've got a good plan. What about Cathal Brugha?"

"We head there."

Her eyes rounded. "We do?"

"The Real IRA's goal is to push British military control out of Northern Ireland, which—"

INITIUM

"Makes the barracks the most likely targets." Ms. Bridges nodded.

"If they're headed to Ballykelly, there's time."

Throwing the map into the backseat, Ms. Bridges started the engine and hit the accelerator, jerking the car into the street. Fifteen minutes later, they were parked along the street across from the barracks. On the way there, Ms. Bridges made two calls on a SAT phone she had tucked under her seat.

A medium drizzle began, blurring their view out the windshield, but not so much that they couldn't see the granite pillars and spiked iron fence protecting the entrance of the army barracks.

"I don't understand why you didn't want the commander to shut down the installation."

Tom unbuckled his seatbelt and zipped up his jacket. "If there's a double agent in the ranks of the RIRA, they'll realize an alert has been issued for these locations. They'll expect increased security. But if we give them an option—"

"That's only going to work if they haven't already been here."

"True." Tom said, opening his door. "Which is why I'm going to take a little walk."

"Wait for me."

"No." The wet rain landed on his neck with a chill. "We can't risk blowing Connor's cover. If he sees me by myself, I may be able to get him to talk to me."

"And if he attacks you, again?"

Tom looked at his battered reflection in the window, then over his shoulder at the red brick fortress housing British soldiers. He glanced back. "I think I'll be okay."

Ms. Bridges twisted her lips, looking unsure.

"What if you take one route and I the other?" he suggested.

With a nod, Ms. Bridges grabbed the SAT phone, stuffing it into her waistband and pulling her sweater down over it, before retrieving her umbrella from the back seat. She stayed in the car until he'd crossed the street. There was an open bakery on the corner and Tom ordered a cup of coffee and a paper, which he used to shield his head as he walked along the south perimeter.

Nothing appeared out of the ordinary, and he only heard the quiet sounds of a Sunday morning. What little pedestrian traffic there was on the street were those grabbing their own coffee or something from the bakery before church—Tom stopped. *Church.*

Turning in a circle, he searched above the building tops for —*there*. Ahead of him was the bell tower of a church. He dumped his coffee into a trashcan and jogged toward it. Rounding the corner, a gray stone church that looked a thousand years old stood before him. A sign surrounded by a flowerbed of white roses welcomed members and visitors to Cathal Protestant Parish.

Among the Real IRA's objections was a battle of religion. Irish Catholics versus Irish Protestants, influenced by the British and spurring the paramilitary's resentment. Tom searched the streets, eying several cars parked nearby. His heart pounded in his chest. Were any of them armed with a bomb?

There was only one way to find out. Tom continued his stroll, passing the first car, a red one similar to the vehicle in Omagh, but a different make. He didn't see anything suspicious visible through the windows. Didn't mean there wasn't anything in the trunk.

There was no way to check that, so he had to keep going. When he got to the fourth car, he paused. In the backseat was a box with the top opened just enough that he could glimpse a bundle of wires. Tom looked around, pulse pounding in his ears.

INITIUM

It was still early so no one was in church yet, but it wouldn't be long before that changed. Tom retraced his steps quickly. He had to get help. He was nearly around the corner when something hard hit him from behind, throwing him to the street just as an explosion erupted, rattling every bone in his body. The muted sound of metal crashing, glass breaking, and car alarms were all he could hear past the ringing in his ears.

Tom twisted to his side, every muscle sore and his head throbbing in time with...sirens. Those were sirens.

"Walsh! Walsh!" His name barely registered in his ears. He turned his head to see Ms. Bridges racing toward him.

"Anything broken?"

Ms. Bridges knelt next to him and waited for him to do a quick mental inventory of any pain he was feeling before he shook his head. *That hurt.* He let her help him up. An ambulance and two police cars sped by, halting just shy of where he'd been standing before he'd taken the hit.

"What happened?"

"A bomb in the car by the church." His voice echoed in his head like a gong. "I was coming to tell you, but it exploded."

"You mean you were just enjoying a Sunday morning walk, right?" Tom saw her gesture with a subtle tilt of her head to the Gardaí walking towards them. "Keep it simple and they won't press for more information. We'll want to get back to the scene, eh."

Tom didn't need to be told how to create a story. Twenty minutes later, he and Ms. Bridges had answered all the Gardaí's questions and even agreed to allow the medic to check him out. When he was done, he pulled on his coat and paused when his fingers traced the pocket, hearing the crinkle of something inside.

He frowned. Slipping his hand inside, he palmed a piece of paper that hadn't been there before. He kept it hidden away as they walked as quickly as he could manage without getting dizzy.

Ms. Bridges put her hand on his arm when he started to sway. "Whoa, the car's not goin' anywhere."

Tom looked over his shoulder and then around them, searching among the trees, buildings, and walkways. "Murphy was here."

"What?" She hissed, looking around with him. "Where? When?"

"Just before the blast. Someone shoved me around the corner of that building. It had to be him."

"And you let him get away?"

Tom looked at her like she was crazy. He balled his fist then flicked his fingers out. "Explosion."

She narrowed her eyes on him. "You sure it wasn't a favor? Your mate saves you and you let him go?"

"No." He reached into his pocket, pulling out the piece of paper and unfolding it. It was a single line—an address.

"But I think he gave me the location of where to find him."

CHAPTER FOURTEEN

SEPTEMBER 1, 1998
Dublin, Ireland

"YOU'RE SURE ABOUT THIS?" Ms. Bridges asked Tom as she handed him her SAT phone. He took it and put it in the generic gray backpack they'd purchased from a nearby shop before returning to her apartment. He arched an eyebrow.

"Are you?"

"No." She crossed her arms, and leaned back into her secondhand chair, scowling. "But I guess my director knows better than me. Sending some American into my investigation. It's rubbish."

Tom understood her frustration. "I'm not taking over your investigation. You're going to have to trust me, Ms. Bridges."

"Trust you, ha!" Ms. Bridges leaned forward, pressing her palms flat against the table between them. "You won't even call me by my first name."

Zipping the bag, he pulled it over his shoulder. "I call you

Ms. Bridges because I respect you, your position in MI5, and because I unequivocally respect the woman I love back home. You are a professional and as such should always be treated like one when you're in the field."

Ms. Bridges opened her mouth, then closed it, a small wrinkle forming between her brows before Tom caught a slight glistening in her eyes. He knew it wasn't easy for women to make their place in the CIA and he imagined it was probably the same in MI5.

"I'll call as soon as I can."

"Be safe." Ms. Bridges walked him to the door of the tiny apartment. "And Mr. Walsh," She paused. "Watch out for that right hook, eh?"

"Will do." Tom hustled down the stairs, anxious to get to the address Sean had given him. After leaving the Cathal Brugha, someone from MI5 had called and identified Connor Murphy through video surveillance taken from the army barracks. Had Sean set that bomb up? The protestant church probably served the British military, who was likely the intended target of the Real IRA. So why then had Sean detonated it when no one was at the church yet?

Tom nearly cursed when a white Vauxhall Cavalier pulled up next to the apartment building. Except for the color, and maybe year, the four-door sedan Ms. Bridges had arranged to take him to the address Sean gave him was the same model of the vehicle used in the Omagh bombing. He climbed into the passenger seat, praying this wasn't a bad omen.

THE PORTLY MAN driving extended a hand and Tom shook it, both exchanging a greeting before he began driving.

"Had to look this place up."

INITIUM

Tom looked at the driver's ID hanging from the mirror. Arwal Shannon. "How far is it you think?"

"Eh, a bit outside the city." Arwal eyed him. "You on holiday then?"

Tom only nodded before asking the one thing the Irish never get tired of discussing. Looking out of his window at the sky he said, "You think it's going to rain today?"

That was all it took. Arwal chatted without much prompting for the entirety of the trip. His words came to a halt when the car did, next to a two-story stone cottage near St. Margaret's.

Tom handed over the fare plus a tip that brought a smile to Arwal's face.

"Wait." Arwal reached into the seat behind him and pulled out an umbrella. "The sky looks soft now, but ya never know when she'll get squally."

Refusing the umbrella would be insulting so Tom accepted it with a smile. "Thank you."

Arwal tipped his head. "*Slán leat.*"

After wishing his driver safety and health as well, Tom faced the home. The smell of wood smoke pulled his gaze to the chimney, from which a plume curled into the air. Hesitation slowed his steps toward the house. What was he walking into? Was this a safehouse for the CIA?

His question remained unanswered when an older woman with gray hair swept up into a low bun opened the door. Weary eyes took him in as she ran her weathered hands across the apron she wore, leaving a trail of white dust behind. Flour, he guessed, based on the inviting aroma of fresh bread wafting from the home.

They both just stood there, neither, it seemed, wanting to reveal their hand but when the echo of a cry erupted behind her, the cautious stand-off ended.

"Come." The woman said.

Shutting the door behind him, the woman ushered him into the open living space. A fire crackled, sparks spitting from the stone fireplace centering the room. To his left was a kitchen where mounds of raw dough were prepped for the oven.

"Sit. I'll have your tea and some breakfast for you."

Before Tom could tell her that wasn't necessary, the woman disappeared up the creaky wooden stairs with the agility of someone much younger. Tom tried hard not to think about how odd it was that she didn't ask for his name; she'd simply invited him in and offered him breakfast as if he'd been expected. He looked around the quaint home. Aged beams, heavy curtains, and the heat radiating from the fire and the oven made the home feel comfortable.

The thick oak, front door swung open and the bearded man from last night stood there. Hooded eyes that held a thousand years of heartache met Tom's, and he saw his friend.

"Sha—Connor?"

"You look terrible, mate." The Irish brogue came so natural to Sean. That, combined with his reddish hair, had made him the ideal candidate to infiltrate the Real IRA for the CIA. He closed the door behind him.

Tom blinked, the comment taking him off guard. "Thanks to you."

The sound of squeaking floorboards announced the elderly woman's return. She took Sean's coat and busied herself in the kitchen with a tea kettle. A moment later, she brought it over to the table, poured two cups of tea and added cream before bringing a plate of warm bread and butter to them. Once more she climbed the stairs, leaving Tom and Sean to their meal.

"You left." There was a growl in Sean's voice. "I tried to make contact but no one would take my calls. I went to the office and everyone was gone."

INITIUM

"I'm sorry. I tried to talk Jennings out of leaving but—"

"You thought I was responsible." The weight of his words hung heavy in the air. "You thought I allowed that bomb into Omagh."

Sean's voice cracked and Tom swallowed the ache, not wanting to imagine how much worse it was for his friend.

"No. I never thought that. It's why I'm here to bring you back so you can explain to Jennings and—"

"No." Sean rose to his feet and began pacing. "I'm not leaving until I can prove my innocence."

"Who bombed Omagh?"

"Rònán O'Hagan."

Tom breathed out slowly. "You're sure?"

"Ay."

Shortly after the Good Friday Agreement was signed bringing a ceasefire to the North Ireland peace process, Rònán O'Hagan was ousted from the Provisional IRA and began his own operation, attracting disgruntled members to form what is now the Real IRA. He was also rumored to be behind the orders for multiple bombings at British military installations that took the lives of a dozen soldiers and four civilians. It was why Tom and the CIA were in Ireland. Stop O'Hagan and prevent the Real IRA from continuing its deadly mission.

"He wasn't working alone."

Tom suspected that. O'Hagan used ranking members to do his dirty work so that his hands were always clean. The CIA had hoped Sean's placement would give them the evidence they'd needed but then...Omagh.

"Sean, they have photos of you driving the car days before the bombing. And this morning? Somebody could've been killed. I could've been killed."

"I made sure you were safe."

Tom pointed to his face. "And last night?"

"You made a nuisance of yourself at the pub, lad."

"I was leaving."

"But ye got the attention of Maxwell and he's the one who pushed us this morning."

"Is that why you hit me?"

"I was mad." Sean's eyes became slits. "And you should know how to defend yourself."

"I wasn't expecting my friend to break my nose."

Several seconds spread between them before a sharp wail pulled both their attentions to the elderly woman holding a bundle in her arms. On the last step she looked up, a sad smile on her lips. She walked to Sean and placed the bundle in his arms.

Sean moved the blanket to reveal the cherub face of an infant. Tom had never seen a baby so small. Pink cheeks, tiny nose, it was like a doll. He frowned. "I don't understand."

Without a word, the woman went to the stove and removed the pot holding a bottle inside. She tested the milk on her wrist before bringing it to Sean just as the child began to whimper.

"The baby is yours?"

"Ay."

"But I..." he swallowed. Annie and the baby had been listed as dead. Had the authorities gotten it wrong? Was it a mistake? Was Annie alive?

"I see her eyes." Sean's words were low, melodic even. "Annie's. The babe's too young to smile but I imagine it'll be Annie's too."

A lump of emotion burned Tom's throat. *Annie hadn't made it.* "I'm sorry, Sean."

Sharp eyes, green as the fields outside, landed on him. "I meant what I said last night. You're to leave and never come back."

Tom frowned. "Sean, we need to talk to Director Jennings."

INITIUM

Let him know you are alive. We'll bring you back and..." his eyes fell to the child.

"It's too dangerous." Sean's harsh tone startled the baby whose closed eyelids squished tight, lip puckering. He soothed the baby with a gentle rock.

"You want to know why I wasn't there in Omagh that morning, why I was at the church this morning? I was looking for evidence."

"Evidence?"

"When I said O'Hagan isn't working alone, I didn't mean with the Real IRA. There's been an increase in attacks against the Gardaí and British military because someone is providing weapons and money. Jennings wanted me to find out who, but O'Hagan started to become suspicious when the RUC raided that home in Meigh. He suspected RUC had placed a double agent among the group, so he used Omagh as a test."

He glanced down at the baby resting in his arms. "They were watching me. Waiting for my reaction when news reached me that Annie had been caught in the explosion. As far as they know the baby died along with her, but," he swallowed, "there was a nurse, someone from our church, she recognized Annie and..." His voice grew rough. "She gave me a piece of my heart back."

Tom swallowed hard against the lump of emotion balling in his throat. His heart squeezed at the suffering Sean had to face on his own and it reaffirmed his mission here. He'd found Sean and now he'd do whatever it took to bring him and his child back to the U.S. Would Jennings help him if he knew the truth behind Sean's absence that morning in Omagh? The anger Tom felt when they left Ireland returned. If Jennings wouldn't help, then he'd call Reuben for a favor.

"I have a friend who can help get you out of here."

"I'm not leaving." Sean placed the baby against his chest

and started patting. "My job's not done here. My wife was murdered. So were others. And until I find the person responsible for bringing that bomb—"

"You already said it's O'Hagan." Tom slid forward in his chair. "We can give that information to the CIA." He kept Ms. Bridges and MI5 to himself. "Or the Gardaí. I can help you arrange—"

"It's not just O'Hagan." Sean's hand stopped its rhymical pat. "I was there when a shipment of weapons arrived from the Balkins. Rifles, grenade launchers, explosives. They're planning another attack. Bigger than Omagh and someone outside of Ireland is brokering the deal." He snapped his lips closed, the vein in his neck pumping.

"I won't let them destroy anyone else's life."

Sean rose from his chair, tucking the blanket around the baby. He opened the front door and Tom expected to be asked to leave, but Sean stepped out and was gone for half a minute before he returned with a blackened canister. He set it on the table in front of Tom.

"This morning the bomb went off early. I don't think it was an accident."

Tom picked up the damaged piece of metal, realizing what it was—ordnance. The remains had flecks of yellow paint forming nearly unreadable letters that Tom recognized.

U.S. Army.

"You got this from the explosion today?"

"No."

The baby began to whimper, and Sean swayed. "I picked that up from the botched explosion outside of Ebrington Barracks in Derry a month ago."

Tom rubbed his thumb against the canister. "You think someone from the U.S. is involved?"

"I don't know, but I ain't leavin' till I find out."

INITIUM

The implication of what Sean was saying sat heavily on Tom's chest. It was unbelievable. Given all that was happening with the recent embassy bombings there was no way the U.S. would allow their weapons to fall into the hands of the Real IRA. They were engaging in terrorism just like al-Qaeda, and the U.S. would not support it.

He eyed the canister on the table—so how did something like this get into Rònán O'Hagan's possession?

Sean had moved to an upholstered rocker near the fireplace while Tom was examining the exploded ordnance and had begun humming a low lullaby for his baby. *His heart.* The only thing he had left of his Annie. Tom watched him rock his child and prayed. First for Sean's loss, and then for forgiveness.

Because once again, he was going to break his promise to Sam.

CHAPTER FIFTEEN

SEPTEMBER 3, 1998
London, England

TOM USED the van's sideview mirror to keep an eye on the car trailing them. Ms. Bridges was doing a good job keeping her distance, but he could still spot the small, gray vehicle popping in and out of view as they drove past London's Hyde Park.

"You think she can handle this?" Sean asked from the driver's seat.

"She's got as much invested in this as we do." He regretted the words, sliding a look at Sean. No one had more invested in this plan working than him. "We could let MI5 handle this. Get you and the baby out of Ireland."

Sean's hands tightened over the steering wheel. "I want to look him in the eyes."

It had been five days since Tom walked into that cottage, discovering not just his friend still alive, but his daughter too. With the help of Ms. Bridges, he and Sean had spent the next

INITIUM

few days creating a plan that they hoped would not only draw O'Hagan out, but also whoever was behind supplying American weapons to the Real IRA.

Using his position, Sean sent a message to O'Hagan saying he'd connected with an arms dealer who could provide their group with a cache of weapons their current supplier couldn't. The caveat was that Tom—who'd be playing the part of arms dealer—wanted to meet O'Hagan in person first. To sweeten the deal, Tom offered the first shipment free of charge, as a goodwill gesture.

Goodwill gesture—what a crock. There was nothing benevolent about what these weapons would be used for, but it was enough to get O'Hagan to agree.

"I'm not going back." Sean steered the van alongside the train tracks. "Once I clear my name and put whoever is behind Omagh in jail, I'm taking us..." he blew out a breath. "Somewhere."

"What about your parents? Sister? They'll help you. Sam and I can help you with the baby."

"I know they will, and I appreciate what you're saying but I can't go back. Annie and I made all these plans, and going back without her...I need to go somewhere new. Have a fresh start."

Tom couldn't voice an argument. After falling for Sam, he couldn't imagine life without her, which had made this last week that much harder. He hadn't been able to reach her and could only guess that her job had called her away.

"You ever ask your girl to marry you?"

"As soon as I got home. Still can't believe she agreed." He thought about his unanswered calls. "Hoping she hasn't changed her mind."

"If she's smart, she will."

The tease in Sean's voice was the first semblance of the

friend Tom remembered. He allowed himself a brief smile before asking, "And Annie's family?"

"She doesn't have any siblings and her parents are older. Until I know for certain they wouldn't be in danger, it's better if we stay away."

Sean pulled next to a secured fence close to a railyard and stopped the van. "If everything today goes as planned then hopefully—" his gaze followed a freight train moving slowly along the tracks—"it won't be too long before we can visit."

In danger. Tom thought about the church explosion. Sean learned someone named Niall transposed the timer on the bomb setting it off too early. His mistake saved lives...if it was in fact, a mistake. "You sure you trust O'Hagan to show up?"

Sean snorted. He picked up a black zippered case and opened it, then pulled out an earwig and placed it in his ear. "Not as far as I can throw him, but he's got a chip on his shoulder as big as the Blarney Stone and he means to make a name for himself."

He nodded toward the wooden crates stacked in the back of the van. "We're giving him that chance."

"You think it'll bring out the supplier?" Tom took the zippered case and selected his own earwig.

"I told ya," Sean said, slipping back into his Irish brogue. "O'Hagan's got a bit of a pride problem. Few rumors here and there about our great leader's brilliance switching to a new dealer'll put a bit o' pressure on him. And I have no doubt he's made a call. He'll make sure *someone* delivers."

"Coms check." Ms. Bridges' voice echoed in their ears. "Team's in place and ready."

"Coms good." Tom and Sean answered together.

"No changes?" Tom asked.

"No. We'll wait until the exchange is made and then track

INITIUM

the subjects when they leave. London Police will make the arrest."

Sean's mobile phone rang. Tom listened to the one-word response, waiting for the thumbs up signaling that they were a go. It didn't come. An unsettled feeling started growing in Tom's stomach as a frown darkened his friend's expression.

"We may have a problem."

Sean set the phone down and started the van back up. "O'Hagan changed the location of the meet. A warehouse in Tottenham."

"What's in Tottenham?"

"Dodgy people." Ms. Bridges answered Tom, her English accent heavy in their earpiece. "You have an address?" Sean told her and she muttered a curse that had him sending Tom a wide-eyed look. "There's no way I can get a team there in time. You have to delay or—"

"We can't." Tom and Sean said at the same time.

"If we give O'Hagan a reason to be suspicious, he'll call it." Sean accelerated. "And it won't matter what we promise him, he won't trust me again. This is our chance."

"Ms. Bridges why don't you hang back." Tom said. "It's likely O'Hagan will have eyes on the location and we don't want to alert him to your presence."

"Good point. If you boys can keep them talking, I'll work on finding another way in and getting backup to meet me."

Sean gave an imperceptible nod and in the sideview mirror, Tom watched Ms. Bridges cut left. They were on their own now.

Tom braced himself against the pot-hole-strewn road. He didn't like the sudden change in plans, especially without having backup. The van bounced over a worn grade crossing, and along a rutted road until he found an access point to enter a railyard lined by old warehouses. Graffiti was the only pop of color against the brown and beige, windowless structure that Sean had been instructed to meet at.

Sean drove around the abandoned building and backed the van into the darkened warehouse, then cut the engine. He and Tom gave each other a look before exiting the van. There was no sound of life apart from their footsteps and the van's settling engine. A chill cut down Tom's spine. Were they walking into a trap?

The entire space was filled with old machinery, boxes, and tons of discarded newspapers. Tom breathed in the smell of ink, his foot stepping on a faded, grime-covered front page of *The London Post*. A fluttering noise overhead—likely a disgruntled pigeon—pulled Tom's attention upward. He searched the catwalk and prayed Ms. Bridges was making progress.

The perimeter search complete, Tom met Sean at the back of the van just as the screech of rusted metal alerted them to a second door being opened on the opposite side of the warehouse. A gray car rolled in through the entrance slowly as the obvious hired gun who'd rolled the door opened stood guard.

"Recognize him?" Tom said without moving his lips.

Sean gave subtle shake of his head, his attention holding steady on the middle-aged man emerging from the car.

"Murphy." O'Hagan addressed Sean and then turned to Tom. The thug was a lot skinnier than Tom had pictured. O'Hagen was pale, with blond hair on the greasy side. Nothing like the meaty goons to his right and left. He came closer and eyed Tom's face.

"What 'appened to you?"

"You wanted to know if we could trust him." Sean shrugged. "Fists don't lie."

"Oi, you did that, did ya' Murphy?" O'Hagan pressed a fist to his lips, laughing. Then he threw a quick couple of air jabs at Sean, who dutifully played along.

INITIUM

"A'right, let's see the goods shall we?"

Tom stepped aside, keeping count of the men. Two with O'Hagan, a driver, and one standing sentry. Sean opened the van's back door revealing the stack of crates he and Tom had loaded in there earlier. He lifted a cover and stood back. O'Hagan leaned forward and whistled as he reached in and pulled out the grenade launcher. His eyes gleamed with the kind of excitement a child had when they got to the prize in the bottom of the cereal box.

"Well, well, well." He placed the weapon on his shoulder, looking every bit the deranged terrorist. "Where'd you get 'em?"

"Hang tight." Ms. Bridges' whispered through their coms. "We've got patrols marking the perimeter a half mile out, but we have a blind spot. A road on the backside. A bit rural and covered with trees. We can't get sights on the warehouse without—"

Tom crossed his arms over his chest, tuning out Ms. Bridges' explanation. "Does it matter? If you don't want them, I've got another buyer lined up."

"Didn't say that, did I?" O'Hagan replaced the weapon and rubbed the scruff on his chin, looking Tom over. "What 'bout explosives?"

Tom noticed Sean's hands curl into fists slightly before relaxing.

"What's the job?" Sean asked.

"What's it to you?" O'Hagan snarled. "You got a conscience?"

"No, but I need to know how much. Type. You planning to take out a car or a bridge?"

O'Hagan sniffed, shaking his head. "I don't like the smell of this." He turned. "I'm out."

"What d'ya mean?" Sean started forward, but froze the instant the goons pulled guns from their waistbands.

"What is this?" Tom asked, putting as much indignation into his voice as possible. He turned his glare on Sean. "Thought you told me this guy was a serious buyer."

"Look," Sean said to O'Hagan. "You wanted grenade launchers and I got them for ya, mate."

"And now I'm telling ya I want explosives. When ya' get 'em have Stevens call me. And make sure he gets the location right next time. I don't like jumping over hill and dale."

Sean shot a look back at Tom, the confusion plain as day in his eyes. If O'Hagan hadn't changed the location; Tom's eyes snapped to the catwalk in time to see a man step out of the shadows.

His warning was cut off by gunfire and O'Hagan's scream as he dropped to the ground, blood spilling from his leg. O'Hagan's men pulled him to cover behind fifty-gallon steel drums and returned fire. Sean grabbed Tom and threw him around the side of the van as more shots ricocheted off the metal.

"We've got gunfire." Tom pressed his back to the van, heart pounding. "One hit to O'Hagan, at least four active shooters." He felt Sean tap his arm and hold up his hand, bloody fingers splayed. "Five, five—"

Tom stopped talking, his eyes following Sean's hand. His friend's stomach that was covered in blood.

"Murphy's shot," he shouted, pulling off his jacket at the same time. "I repeat. Murphy's been shot."

CHAPTER SIXTEEN

SEPTEMBER 3, 1998
London, England

"MS. BRIDGES, WHERE ARE YOU?" Tom cradled Sean, carefully lowering him to the ground. A small explosion erupted to his left. Acting on instinct, he curled his body over Sean's as smoke and a chemical odor filled the air. He had to get Sean out of here.

"Ms. Bridges!"

Tom pulled out his earpiece. Was it even working? Sean groaned, pressing Tom's jacket to his bloody abdomen. Gun shots to the gut were never good. Tom coughed and looked over his shoulder toward the nearest exit. He needed to pull Sean outside, but all he could think about was the puddle of blood staining the pages of a newspaper.

"Can you hear me, Bridges?"

Sean shook his head, breath rattling between lips wet with spittle. "Dead."

Tom sucked in a breath. "What?"

Tapping his ear, Sean gave him a painful grimace. "Earpiece, not girl."

Tom squeezed Sean's shoulder. "Help is on the way. Hang in there."

Mixed in with the sounds of bullets hitting concrete and metal, Tom could hear O'Hagan screaming for help.

Sean sputtered, and a trickle of blood mixed with spit filled the corner of his lips. "Go...get...Ha...Ha..."

"I'm not leaving you." Tom shook his head. Let O'Hagan's men grab him. Or let him bleed out. He couldn't care less either way. He wasn't leaving Sean.

"He's the...only one." Sean rasped. "Knows the...American."

Tom peered around the tire. O'Hagan had been pulled clear of the black vehicle and over to a stack of crates, where one of the goons was returning fire on the catwalk shooter. Even if Tom left Sean there was no way he could make it there without getting shot himself.

Who were the gunmen? Why were they shooting at O'Hagan?

Pushing himself back, he shook his head at Sean. "It's not worth it. I'm getting us out of here—"

"Please. You can't...let 'im..." Sean sucked in a breath, his face paling. "For Annie."

"Don't ask me to do this." Tom choked on the black smoke. "You have a baby."

Sean lifted Tom's jacket from his wound, assessed it, and then looked up, eyes glistening. He offered a sad smile.

"Stop 'em, Tom. Make..." he wheezed. "Make the...world better." He coughed and more blood dripped from his lip. "Safer."

INITIUM

"No. You're going to do that." Tom's voice was desperate. "Stay with me. You're going to—"

Another explosion rocked the building, the stench of rubber and gasoline filling the air.

Sean grabbed his arm and Tom met his friend's anguished gaze.

"Get O'Hagan." Sean grabbed at his neck, fingers wrapping around a chain, yanking it free and pressing it into Tom's hand. "Get truth."

Sean blinked and a tear slipped out just before the life left his green eyes. The gunshots around them were slowing down...or maybe that was just the trauma of watching his friend die in front of him. A grunting noise pulled Tom's attention to O'Hagan who was trying to crawl to safety, a gun in his hand, likely from the muscle, who was now sprawled out and laying lifeless on the concrete.

Slowly, Tom became aware of sirens in the distance. Bridges was sending help. Tom closed his fist around Sean's trinity knot pendent and shoved it in his pocket, before rising to his feet.

O'Hagan caught sight of him and half-whispered-half-yelled, "Help me."

A nearby pile of overturned crates would give Tom just enough cover he could army crawl to O'Hagan. He forced himself to move. He wouldn't let Sean's death be in vain. Shimmying across the floor, Tom could hear the lick of flames and feel the heat radiating from what remained of O'Hagan's car. Crawling the last foot, he found O'Hagan curled in the fetal position, gun shaking in his hands.

He aimed it at Tom. "I'll shoot ye' if you don't help me."

"If you shoot me, we'll both die in here." Tom surveyed the bloody mess that was once O'Hagan's knee.

O'Hagan dropped his arm and let out a frustrated cry. "Fine."

Tom took the gun and tucked it into his waistband. Casting a quick look-over to where the metal staircase was leading from the catwalk. Empty.

"We've got to hurry."

"Bloody Stevens! No good, double-crossing piece of—"

"That the guy shooting at you?" Tom slipped his arm beneath O'Hagan's back to lift him off the ground.

"Bruh, he's shootin' at us both." O'Hagan chuckled grimly. "Got Connor, did he?"

Tom wanted to drop the man right there. "Who's Stevens? Why'd he want Murphy dead?"

"You don't cut into a man's bread and butter and expect to get away." O'Hagan grimaced as Tom pulled him to his feet. "Oi mate, I got me a bad leg."

"He's your supplier?"

"Not anymore." O'Hagan laughed and Tom expected shock was setting in. If he was going to get any intel, he'd need to get it fast.

"Stevens' his first or last name?"

"Last." A voice said from behind.

Tom turned slowly, supporting O'Hagan, and met the steely-eyed gaze of the man called Stevens. O'Hagan went rigid and then suddenly seemed far too heavy, as if the weight of impending death was too much for him to hold up. He slipped in Tom's grip.

"You gonna kill me, mate?" O'Hagan sagged a little lower. "I saved your life."

Stevens laughed. "I got my orders."

O'Hagan seemed to rally at that. He grunted as he pressed into Tom and forced himself upward. "He's here."

Stevens stayed quiet but his gaze flicked up and to the left.

INITIUM

Tom's breathing slowed. Was the American supplier here? It was then that he noticed Stevens wasn't the man he'd seen on the catwalk. Too skinny, shorter. Tom checked his peripheral, searching for any sign of the other shooter.

Stevens moved the rifle between them. "Who's first then?"

Under the pretense he was unable to hold O'Hagan up any longer, Tom let the man slip to the floor and reached for the gun in his waistband, but O'Hagan was quicker. He grabbed for it first, knocking Tom sideways in the process. The echo of the shots was deafening. O'Hagan crumpled without a cry, his gun clattering across the cement.

Stevens stumbled sideways before turning his gun on Tom. He took one hand off the rifle and touched his shoulder. When he pulled his fingers away, they were red. "Guess I deserved that, eh?"

Tom eyed the gun near his foot. He wasn't faster than a bullet.

Lord, I could use some help. He could still hear approaching sirens. Close, but not close enough to stop Stevens' finger from pulling the trigger. His eyes reflected the dance of the fire making its way towards them.

This was it. He'd failed his mission to bring Sean home and he had broken his vow to Sam. He wasn't going to make it back to her after all. *Lord, forgive me.*

A spray of cold water burst from the overhead fire suppression system, raining down on the men. Stevens looked up, the barrel of the rifle angling up and to the right as his sights shifted. Tom took advantage of the distraction, grabbed for the weapon, and pulled the trigger.

CHAPTER SEVENTEEN

2020

Austin, Texas

TOM HAD NEVER BEEN MORE grateful to step out of the muggy afternoon and into the air-conditioned headquarters for the Texas Rangers. He chuckled to himself as he walked past men carrying cowboy hats and wearing star shaped badges rather than baseball bats and ball caps.

One of those men, an older one with stark white hair and a mustache that gave off serious Sam Elliott vibes met him in the hallway with a handshake. Dressed in a pair of starched jeans and a crisp white collared shirt, the former Texas Ranger looked far more comfortable than Tom was in his D.C. suit.

"Tom Walsh, good to finally meet you, sir." Officer Jackson Crawford had at least twenty plus years on Tom, but his grip was stronger than a lot of guys half his age. "Find the place alright?"

INITIUM

"Sure did." Tom said. "Austin might be competing with D.C. for worst traffic."

"I don't doubt that." Officer Crawford laughed. "I appreciate you getting here on such short notice. I was told you might be interested in a man of this caliber."

"You were told right."

Tom had walked out of a meeting with the president's security advisor yesterday with three missed calls, four texts, and two emails about a man who had committed at least three felonies against the federal government.

"Anyone else here yet?"

"Oh yeah," Officer Crawford led Tom down the hall. "FBI showed up about an hour ago, and then a young woman with the fiercest set of blue eyes I've ever seen moseyed in here ten minutes ago. She's waiting her turn in the conference room."

Crawford pointed to a room with a sign next to the door marked Interrogation Room 1. "Your man is in there but," he leaned in, his weathered skin at the edge of his eyes crinkling in a conspiratorial look. "I can give you a little peek-see...find out what you're up against if you like?"

Tom smiled, liking this man. "I won't say no to that."

He followed Officer Crawford into an unmarked room. It was dark, with the only light coming through the one-way mirror, giving Tom his first in-person glimpse of Kekoa Young. Tom let out a low whistle. The file he'd read on the flight over containing Kekoa's official DA photo in his Navy uniform did not adequately portray the solidly built man in a tank top and bright turquoise Hawaiian print shorts sitting at the metal table.

And it seemed, based on the wavy locks of hair touching his shoulder, that Kekoa had fully embraced his separation from the military.

With him was an FBI agent, sitting with his back to the mirror, doing his best to make a dent in Kekoa's smug bearing.

"Federal charges, Mr. Young." The agent said. "You hacked into a high security *federal* prison, accessed their cameras and computer system, and risked exposing the identity of an intelligence officer."

Kekoa Young appeared to try for a humble smile, but it was clear he was proud of what he considered a list of his accomplishments. According to the file Tom had read, Mr. Young was honorably discharged after fulfilling his obligation to the United States Navy as a cryptologist, less than a month ago. He had used his proficient cyber-hacking skills to help apprehend a member of the Mexican cartel responsible for killing an undercover federal agent and kidnapping a CIA officer with the intent to murder her. According to Tom's old friend, Bob Perkins, Mr. Young's *assistance* was unsanctioned and therefore illegal.

Which, apparently, was the route the FBI was trying to use to convince him to join their agency. *Avoid federal charges by using your skillset for good—join the FBI.* It made for a delightful recruitment slogan.

Next to him, Officer Crawford shook his head. "It's like I tell my great nephew, you can't win the game unless you know who you're playing against."

Tom liked this man. "You mentioned he stopped an international extortion ring?"

"Yes, sir." Officer Crawford crossed his arms. "Two days ago, Tank Nash received a phone call from someone who said his daughter, Morgan, had been in a serious car accident. Tank raced out of the house not even letting Jenny—that's his wife—know where he was going. The caller kept him on the phone, letting Tank know the police were already on the scene and not to hang up. Tank was out of his mind sick trying to get to Morgan. Jenny called the local police worried about Tank and that he wouldn't answer her calls. Kept going to voicemail.

INITIUM

Local police didn't think much of it but after about an hour and a half of not hearing from him, Jenny drives to the station and demands to talk to the police chief. She's got one of them new cell phones that lets you track your family members and shows the chief that Tank's been driving all over the place and something isn't right. Chief sends out several officers to the location where Tank's at and they find him in the Wal-Mart parking lot where he's just purchased his third money order."

"Money order?" Tom frowned. "For what?"

"When the police find Tank, the man's a wreck, can hardly speak. Demands to know where Morgan is. Took an officer driving Tank to the restaurant where Morgan works to finally accept she was okay."

"So it was a scam," Tom said, shaking his head.

"The caller used the story about an accident to get Tank out of his house, then once he was on his way changed the story to say that he had kidnapped Morgan and would hurt her unless Tank wired him money.

"They kept him on the phone threatening to hurt her if he hung up, so he did what they said." Officer Crawford's expression darkened. "Tank was so distraught the officers on the scene thought he might have a heart attack."

On the other side of the glass, the FBI agent pushed back from the table and stood. "The offer is only good for an hour," he said before walking out. Tom fought the urge to roll his eyes. The FBI had no creativity. Then again, neither did the CIA, he thought as a woman with long, wavy hair, wearing a black skirt and shiny heels, stepped into Interrogation 1. Kekoa's eyes flashed to the pretty intel officer. His brow lifted, a coy smile playing on his lips.

Tom shook his head. Leave it to the CIA to use honey as bait.

"Afternoon, Mr. Young." The woman sat in the empty

chair. "I'm not going to waste your time. I've read your file and your list of accomplishments are impressive. I'm not here to threaten you with jail time, because I believe that would be a waste of your very valuable skillset. I'm here because the CIA needs people like you. Individuals who genuinely care about the welfare of this nation's citizens, and who want to make a difference in the world by using their talents to keep America safe."

Ooh, she was good. If Tom had to guess, he imagined the intel officer had some experience in psychological operations.

Officer Crawford chuckled. "Told ya she had a fire in her."

"You were telling me about how Kekoa helped the Nash family."

"Well, Kekoa's a friend of my great-nephew, Colton. He came for Colton's wedding but stayed in town to help renovate our family ranch into a veteran's home. When Colton heard about what happened, he thought maybe Kekoa could use his skills to track the wire transfers and find out who was behind it. Kekoa gave us some kind of mumbo jumbo about back-tracing or something like that and—"

"And by mumbo jumbo you mean you have no idea what he's talking about."

"Not a lick of it." Officer Crawford shook his head. "Anyway, a day or two later, that young man," he tipped his head to where Kekoa was sitting, still smiling as the CIA rep continued her pitch, "had the account numbers the money was sent to, the names and address on the account, and the video footage of the suspects pulling the money out from the bank in the Dominican."

And according to the report Tom read on the flight, because of Kekoa's work, Interpol assisted the Dominican National Police in making the arrests. Tom studied Kekoa fielding the CIA officer.

INITIUM

"Have you ever had a shoyu chicken?" Kekoa nodded. "So ono. My buddy Colton told me there's a Hawaiian place in Austin that he—"

"No. But I assure you there's most likely a Hawaiian restaurant in D.C." The woman opened a folder and pulled out a sheet. "I know you haven't been home in a while, Mr. Young. If you join the CIA, I will personally speak with the director to find you an assignment close to Hawaii so you can get all of your favorite meals."

Kekoa's relaxed posture stiffened and his smile vanished. It was clear he wasn't about to be fooled. The CIA would promise to *try* and find an assignment that would appeal to its intel officers, but at the end of the day they would be sent wherever the mission took them.

Tom no longer considered the CIA officer a threat. She hadn't really read the file, or if she did, it was a cursory lookover. He pulled out his cell phone and looked something up, then sent a message to Jack back in D.C.

"Looks like it's your turn."

Tom looked up in time to see the annoyed CIA officer exit the interrogation room. Palming his phone, he headed for the door.

"The Texas Rangers don't want him?"

Officer Crawford rocked on the heels of his worn, leather boots. "That young man's above our paygrade or I'd have him roped up and wearing a cowboy hat quicker than a jackrabbit on a date."

Tom chuckled, then moved into the interrogation room and sat across from Kekoa. The man's strength was even more intimidating up close. Tom prayed he'd done his homework correctly.

"Mr. Young, my name is Tom Walsh and I'm going to make this real simple. The FBI is going to offer you a get out of jail free card if you work for them. The CIA is going to offer you numerous opportunities to show off your skillset. I'm here to offer you a team...a family."

The muscles in Kekoa's shoulders relaxed some but his expression was still wary. Would his strategy work?

Tom's cellphone vibrated in his hand and he took a quick look at it. He smiled up at Kekoa.

"I can also offer you this." He slid his phone over. "I heard it's the best."

Kekoa leaned across the table, his large frame defying all logic for how he'd fit into a Navy ship. He looked up, awe in his eyes over the Renegade500 gaming chair Tom just asked Jack to order. The computer specialist who'd helped him deck out the Agency's cyber office with state-of-the art computers had suggested the chair as the ultimate cyber tech throne and Tom hoped it was enough to tip the odds in his favor.

Kekoa slid the phone back to Tom. "And I won't go to jail?"

Pulling the immunity agreement from inside his coat pocket and a pen, Tom slid them across the table. "All you need to do is sign this."

Taking the pen, Kekoa signed the paper. "You can let the FBI and CIA know that I've made my decision." He put the pen down and looked over Tom's shoulder, a line of worry marking his forehead. He rose to his feet. "One last question. Is there a back door for this place? That CIA *wahine* is scary."

CHAPTER EIGHTEEN

SEPTEMBER 10, 1998
Langley, VA

TOM PAUSED at the CIA Memorial Wall, staring at the stars of CIA officers who had died while in service to the agency. The Book of Honor was encased in a steel frame and listed the names of some, while others would remain anonymous—like Sean.

It felt weird to be back. In America. At Langley. Tom still wasn't sure his brain had caught up with all that had taken place. Sean was dead. Stevens had been taken into custody after Tom shot him in the leg, disarming him as Ms. Bridges, MI5, and the London Police arrived.

After a lengthy interrogation, Stevens admitted being the middleman in an arms smuggling operation with American sympathizers. He gave names and, with the help of MI5, Interpol, and the FBI, three arrests were made in Florida. Stevens also offered the name of one person involved in the Omagh bombing, but it wouldn't be long before all involved were brought to justice.

Make the world safe.

Sean's final words were etched in Tom's soul. He pulled the Irish trinity knot from his pocket. He turned it over, reading the inscription on the back. *Psalm* 23. Tom memorized the six verses of that chapter, taking comfort in the promise that God was never far away—even in the midst of evil and death.

Casting a final look over the stars that would gain one more, Tom walked to the elevators. He still had a job to do.

On the sixth floor, Tom surveyed his old office space feeling like it had been months rather than weeks since he walked away from the National Clandestine Service. He made his way to Director Jennings office, finding the door partially opened, and knocked.

"Come in."

Tom stepped into Director Jennings office and was surprised by the level of emotion he still carried from the last time he was here. Frustration, anger, and disappointment. Now, added to that, there was sadness, but also hope. Hope for a future where Sean's death—his sacrifice—would be honored rather than filed away and forgotten.

"I appreciate you seeing me today, sir." Tom exchanged a handshake with his old boss.

"Must be pretty important." Jennings adjusted his tie and sat back at his desk, gesturing Tom to the chair in front of it. "Heard you're supposed to be getting married in a few hours."

"Yes, sir." Tom smiled.

The second he'd seen Sam waiting for him at the airport, he was even more certain that a long engagement wasn't going to work and when he said as much, Sam agreed. This afternoon, with their family and closest friends as witnesses, Tom would marry Sam in a private ceremony at the Library of Congress

INITIUM

followed by a celebratory dinner at DeLuco's Steakhouse. But before Tom could celebrate the beginning of his life with Sam, he needed to fulfill the promise he'd made to Sean.

"I wanted to ask you for a favor."

Jennings didn't hide his surprise. "A favor from me?"

"Well, you and the agency." Tom handed over the file he created with Ms. Bridges. "The intel Sean collected and the recent arrests made by MI5 and the FBI dealt a devastating blow to the Real IRA, but I don't think it's over. In the report are photos of U.S. military grade weapons that we were able to trace back to shipments earmarked for Turkey, UAE, and Saudi."

Jennings picked up the file and thumbed through the pages, pausing occasionally to read or look at the photos. "And the favor?"

"You and I both know the Real IRA isn't a well-organized terror group. Sean believed the only way they could obtain weapons of that caliber was through the hands of someone within the ranks—someone with access. A defense supplier maybe. Or someone within the military." Tom let that settle for a few seconds. "I'm asking you to continue the investigation. The U.S. is supplying billions of dollars in weapons to these countries, we can't afford to let them fall into wrong hands again."

After a few more seconds, Jennings released a sigh. "You know I can't promise anything."

"I do."

Jennings set the file down. "You're an excellent officer, Tom. Director Klein has been made aware of your work in Ireland and thinks you have a long future in the Agency, maybe station chief or director one day. I've been given permission to offer you your job back and—"

"I appreciate the offer, sir, but my reason for leaving the

agency hasn't changed. I went to Ireland with a single-minded mission, bring Sean home." The memory of Sean cradling his baby flashed to mind. "A part of me wants to believe he might still be alive if the red-tape of bureaucracy hadn't tied the CIA's hands, but then I think about what he accomplished in his death and at the end of the day we all want the same thing, to make the world a better—safer—place for future generations."

Jennings remained silent for a few seconds before giving a nod.

"I'll do what I can about continuing the investigation into the arms trafficking. What are you going to do now? More rogue missions?"

Tom thought about the quiet, graveside service in Galway. Besides the pastor, only Ms. Bridges and Tom were there to watch Sean's casket lowered into the ground still freshly churned from Annie's burial a few weeks before. A granite marker with the trinity knot and Sean and Annie's real names would be placed there soon; the only evidence that they were ever in Ireland.

"I hope not rogue." Tom said. "But I do plan on working a few contract jobs."

"Freelance."

"For now."

The flight back to the U.S. gave Tom plenty of time to consider what he wanted his future to be. Reuben Jones and his team had been careless, in his opinion, and it had cost lives. Tom wanted to try things differently; to coordinate strategic options with the help of agencies and specially skilled individuals to neutralize threats.

"Maybe one day in the future you and I will work together again."

"I hope so." Jennings said, sounding like he meant it. He held up a folded piece of cardstock, the emblem of the CIA on

INITIUM

the front. "There'll be a ceremony later this week to recognize Sean's service and sacrifice. Will you be there?"

"No." Tom had said his good-byes in Ireland. "Sam and I will be out of town."

Awareness dawned on Jennings' face. "Right. Well, you'd better get out of here before Sam changes her mind."

Tom thanked Jennings for his time, and his former director promised once more that he'd look into Tom's request, as well as offered his blessings for the marriage. Tom was headed toward the elevator when his cellphone rang. He saw the foreign number and answered.

"Please tell me I'm not interrupting your wedding right now?" came the now-familiar accented voice.

"No, no." Tom chuckled and paused outside the elevator so he wouldn't lose reception. He checked his watch. "I've got a few more bachelor hours left."

"I'm surprised you didn't marry her the second you landed."

"I would've, but Sam isn't fond of airport food and we both wanted our families to be there."

"Oh, I wish I could be there." Ms. Bridges sighed into the phone. "I would love to meet the woman who has challenged me to set the bar a lot higher when it comes to my future husband."

"I'm gonna call that a compliment, Ms. Bridges."

"It is." The sound of a baby wailing echoed in the background. Tom's chest tightened in response. Ms. Bridges made some cooing sounds and the crying softened.

"You know," she said once the baby had quieted. "I'm much more comfortable with terrorists than babies. At least terrorists have demands I can understand."

"I appreciate you handling this." Tom said, wishing things had turned out differently. That it was Sean consoling his infant child and not an MI5 officer. "Has everything been taken care of?"

"Don't worry, Walsh. You go marry that fiancée of yours and let me take care of things over here."

"I can't thank you enough, Ms. Bridges, for helping me. For helping Sean. I am forever in your debt."

"Call me Sophie and we're even."

"If you need anything M—Sophie, please don't hesitate to call me."

Ms. Bridges laughed. "There now. That was hard wasn't it?"

The elevator door opened and Tom was surprised to see Sam step out, her bright smile a beacon of light and comfort that drew him to her immediately. "I have to go now but I do hope we can work together again."

"Congratulations, Walsh."

Tom ended the call and slipped his phone into his pocket.

"What are you doing here?" he asked Sam, as a CIA officer with his nose in a folder two-stepped around them. "Isn't it bad luck to see the bride before the wedding?"

"I had a meeting with Director Klein...." Sam's gray-blue eyes sparkled. "*And* I wanted to make sure you didn't have any second thoughts."

Taking her hand into his, he smiled. "I've been waiting my whole life to marry you. I just had to meet you first."

Sam's lips pressed into a flirtatious smile. "I was talking about the job. Klein told me Jennings was going to offer your job back. What'd you say?"

"That I had other plans."

"Good." Sam interlaced her fingers with his and pressed the elevator button. "Let's go get married."

CHAPTER NINETEEN

2020
Washington, D.C.

TOM SET his office phone back into its cradle. Opening his top drawer, he pulled out four coins and put them in his pocket before gathering his file. He stepped out of his office and surveyed the transformation that turned the eighth floor of the Acacia Building into a state-of-the-art workspace for his new agency.

It had taken more than twenty years of building networks, gathering investors, and working hundreds of missions that took him away from Sam to get to this point. His attention stopped on the conference table at the center of the room where Jack Hudson, Lyla Fox, Nicolás Garcia, and Kekoa Young sat.

Twenty plus years to build a team.

His team. And now they would receive their first assignment since all coming together, and Tom prayed they would be as good together as they were individually.

"Five thousand dollars, Lyla?" Jack looked at the cup of coffee in his hand like he was afraid of it. "Does Walsh know?"

"Does Walsh know what?" Tom asked.

Four faces turned in his direction. Kekoa pointing at Lyla, Garcia staying silent, and Jack sending Lyla a look that said she'd better start talking.

Tom took his seat at the head of the table, finding a mug of coffee the color of caramel waiting for him. It smelled of caramel too. "What's this?"

"A five-thousand-dollar cup of coffee." Jack mumbled. "Lyla's new machine."

"Okay, first," Lyla held up her index finger. "It was only forty-five hundred, I got a deal. *And* I paid for it myself." She added quickly, shooting a nervous look at Tom before holding her own cup of coffee up. "My contribution to our newest member—"

"I don't really drink coffee."

Lyla let out an exasperated sigh. "Fine. Then to our team as a whole. May the caffeine keep us from killing one another." She eyed Kekoa. "Figuratively speaking, of course."

Tom knew Lyla was putting up an act. Kekoa had integrated seamlessly into the team, winning Lyla over instantly.

Tom sipped his coffee and was pleasantly surprised by how much he enjoyed the taste. He cleared his throat and set the cup down. "Lyla, no more unauthorized purchases, even at your own expense."

"Hey, I'm just trying to make everyone's work life easier. No one wants to work with an un-caffeinated me, all I'm saying."

"Truth." Jack and Garcia said at the same time, which earned each of them a side glare from Lyla.

"Okay, well now that we're safe, I'd like to officially

welcome Kekoa to our team. I think he's going to be a tremendous asset, which we'll need for our first assignment."

"Fulcrum." Kekoa blurted out and then covered his mouth, eyes wide. "Sorry, sir."

Tom ignored Lyla's snickering and nodded to Kekoa. "Did you have something to add, Kekoa?"

"Well, sir," Kekoa gestured around the room, his tattoos and muscles on full display. "We keep calling this the conference room, but that's boring and this is nothing like any conference room I've ever worked in, so I think it needs a name. Fulcrum."

"What's a fulcrum?" Jack asked.

"The room where important activity takes place." Kekoa swiveled in his chair. "It's like the CPU of our office."

"The what?" Lyla asked.

"Central Processing Unit." Jack answered.

"It's like the brain." Garcia's voice was quiet. "Most critical organ in the human body."

"Yes, brah." Kekoa held his fist out to Garcia and after a few long seconds Garcia complied with a fist bump back. "You and I are riding the same wave, yeah."

Garcia pressed his lips together and pulled his ballcap lower over his forehead.

Tom nodded. "I like it. Fitting for what I believe is our agency's purpose."

He stood and pulled out the coins in his pocket and began placing them in front of each team member. "We all have different backgrounds and various reasons for why we're sitting here today. This might not be where some of you imagined you'd be, or maybe you think this is exactly what you've been called to do, a way you can continue to serve your country."

Lyla held up her coin. "What does *non timebo mala* mean?"

"I will fear no evil." Garcia's cool tone grabbed everyone's attention. "Psalm 23."

The Latin phrase and Bible verse reference were important to Tom and his vision for the agency, but he had to be honest with them.

"I don't have to tell any of you what kind of evil exists outside of these walls and I know the work we do here won't solve all that's wrong with the world. But my hope is that if we commit ourselves and work together with excellence and integrity to the best of our ability, we can...leave this world a better place."

"To SNAP and protecting the world from itself." Lyla smiled, lifting her coin in the air. "May we neutralize all threats—"

"Foreign and domestic," Kekoa added.

Jack lifted his coin up. "Strategically, and with integrity."

They all looked at Garcia. His eyes bounced between them before he exhaled and raised his coin with the others. "Safely... and with as little jail time as possible."

Lyla burst into laughter first, followed by Jack and Kekoa. Tom reveled in the feeling. This was what he wanted for SNAP. When the laughter slowed, he tapped his knuckles on the table for everyone's attention.

"We have a new assignment," he said. "Let's get started."

ACKNOWLEDGEMENTS AND AUTHOR'S NOTE

Dear readers,

I knew from the very start that I wanted to give you a preview into how the SNAP Agency began and the man behind it. In the creative process I knew I was going to have to dig into Director Walsh's history, which meant going back in time. Researching turned out to be very interesting as I stumbled upon the bombing in Omagh, Ireland, an actual event that fit the timeline I needed. Taking some creative liberties, I crafted a story around the event, taking a few details like the Real Irish Republican Army's involvement, the miscommunicated intel, even the devastating destruction of the bombing that did take the life of a pregnant woman. I have a great deal of respect for authors who write historical or time split stories because it was no easy task keeping track of technology even just thirty years ago. Even so, writing Initium was so much fun and I hope you enjoyed getting to know the genesis of this specialized agency and getting a sneak peek at the amazing team!

Speaking of team, this novella never would've happened

without the enthusiasm of the team at Revell and my agent, Tamela Hancock Murray. I'm so grateful to my editor, Jennifer Lindsay, and to Emilie Haney for her amazing formatting skills. Special thanks to Jennifer Diebel for keeping my Irish elements on point, any mistakes made are my own fault. And to the early readers who made sure this was a story worth sharing, I'm so grateful for your unswerving belief in me. GIJOE and Lil'Joe, thanks for never complaining about the amount of time I spend with fictional characters. And lastly, I'm so thankful to Jesus for allowing me the opportunity to do what I love.

If you read Initium and enjoyed the story, I would love if you'd share your thoughts on Goodreads, Amazon, and with friends!

ABOUT THE AUTHOR

Natalie Walters is the author of Carol Award finalist *Living Lies*, as well as *Deadly Deceit* and *Silent Shadows*. A military wife, she currently resides in Texas with her soldier husband and is a proud mom of three adult kiddos. She has been published in *Proverbs 31* magazine and has blogged for *Guideposts* online. She loves connecting on social media, sharing her love of books, cooking, and traveling. Natalie comes from a long line of military and law enforcement veterans and is passionate about supporting them through volunteer work, races, and writing stories that affirm no one is defined by their past.

Learn more at www.nataliewalterswriter.com.

NATALIE WALTERS NAILS IT WITH LIGHTS OUT—HEART-POUNDING SUSPENSE AND DETAILS SO REAL YOU HAVE TO WONDER WHO SHE'S REALLY WORKING FOR.

—JAMES R. HANNIBALL,
award-winning, bestselling author of *The Paris Betrayal*

To fight the global war on terroism, CIA Analyst Brynn Taylor invited foreign spies into America. Now one of them is missing. To track him down and stop a cyber blackout, she must work with an elite security team--and the ex-boyfriend she betrayed.

PREORDER LIGHTS OUT TODAY!
Available wherever books and eBooks are sold.

NATALIE WALTERS HAS MASTERFULLY WOVEN AN EMOTIONALLY CHARGED SUSPENSE AND LOVE STORY.

— DIANN MILLS,
author of **Burden of Proof**

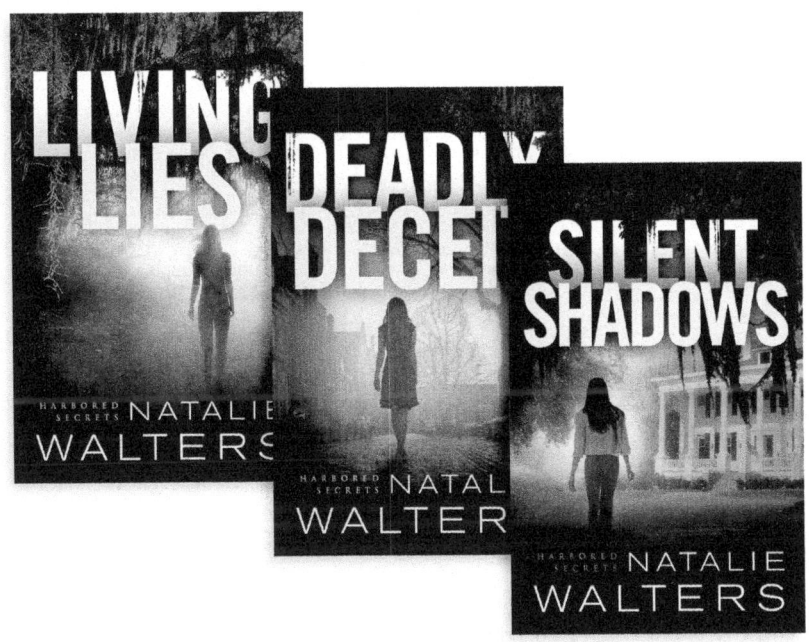

FROM LIVING LIES:

When Lane Kent stumbles across a body in the Georgia woods, she must team up with the town's newest deputy and decide if saving the life of another is worth her darkest secret.

GET THE HARBORED SECRETS SERIES TODAY!

Available wherever books and eBooks are sold.

Made in United States
North Haven, CT
19 October 2022